WHAT WOULD MR DARCY DO?

ABIGAIL REYNOLDS

sourcebooks
landmark

Published by Sourcebooks Landmark, an imprint of Sourcebooks, Inc.
P.O. Box 4410, Naperville, Illinois 60567-4410
(630) 961-3900
FAX: (630) 961-2168
www.sourcebooks.com

Originally published as *From Lambton to Longbourn* in 2001 by Intertidal Press,
Madison, WI

Library of Congress Cataloging-in-Publication Data

Reynolds, Abigail.
  What would Mr. Darcy do? / by Abigail Reynolds.
     p. cm.
  1. Bennet, Elizabeth (Fictitious character)—Fiction. 2. Darcy, Fitzwilliam
(Fictitious character)—Fiction. 3. Gentry—England—Fiction. 4. England—Social
life and customs—19th century—Fiction. I. Austen, Jane, 1775-1817. Pride and
prejudice. II. Title.
  PS3618.E967W47 2011
  813'.6—dc22

                              2010043654

          Printed and bound in the United States of America
              VP 10 9 8 7 6 5 4 3 2 1

To Rebecca,
even if she does like Shakespeare
better than Jane Austen

Chapter 1

ELIZABETH HAD SMILED AT him.

It had been a different sort of smile from the arch one she had worn so many times before. No, this had been a genuine—dare he say affectionate?—smile, something Darcy had despaired of ever seeing. It was only four months since Elizabeth had emphatically rejected his proposal of marriage. She had done more than just reject him, by Jove; she had said he was the last man in the world she could ever be prevailed upon to marry! She had accused him of ungentlemanlike behavior, of cheating a childhood friend, of destroying the happiness of her own sister. Her hands had been clenched, her fine eyes had sparkled with fury.

And yesterday she had smiled at him.

He had not seen her between that horrible evening four long, excruciating months ago and two days previously, when he had returned to Pemberley unexpectedly and found her touring the grounds with her aunt and uncle. Once his shock wore off, he realized that providence was providing him with a second chance. This was his opportunity to show her he had changed, that he was a man worthy of her love. He had done his best, inviting her uncle to fish at Pemberley, introducing her to his sister Georgiana, entertaining them with the very best Pemberley had to offer. And she had smiled at him.

Fitzwilliam Darcy urged his horse into a canter and then jumped over the wide hedge. It would have been much easier to follow the road, but he was too impatient for that. He had been awake for hours, waiting for a civilized hour so he could call on Elizabeth. Once he mounted his horse, he could not hold back any longer. He took the very shortest route from Pemberley to the town of Lambton.

He slowed his horse to a walk on the edge of town, making an extra effort to acknowledge the townsfolk on the street. He had not frequented Lambton in the past, and now this was the second time in three days he had ridden up to the inn on High Street. It would forever be Elizabeth's inn in his mind now. He dismounted and tossed the reins to a lad from the inn. Would Elizabeth smile at him today?

He was greeted by the innkeeper himself. "Mr. Darcy, welcome back to our establishment. It is an honor."

Darcy inclined his head graciously. "Is Miss Bennet within?"

"Indeed, sir, she's right in the private parlour reading some letters. Mr. and Mrs. Gardiner, they walked out to the church a bit ago."

So Elizabeth was alone! This was better than he could have hoped. Would she smile for him today? He allowed a servant to open the parlour door for him, but followed close on his heels.

She did not smile. Instead, she darted from her seat and cried, "Oh! Where, where is my uncle?" Her pale face and impetuous manner made him start, and before he could recover himself enough to speak, she hastily exclaimed, "I beg your pardon, but I must leave you. I must find Mr. Gardiner this moment, on business that cannot be delayed; I have not a moment to lose."

"Good God! What is the matter?" cried Darcy, with more feeling than politeness; then recollecting himself, "I will not detain you a minute, but let me, or let the servant, go after Mr. and Mrs. Gardiner. You are not well enough;—you cannot go yourself."

Elizabeth hesitated, but her knees trembled under her, and she felt how little would be gained by her attempting to pursue them. Calling back the servant, therefore, she commissioned him, though in so breathless an accent as made her almost unintelligible, to fetch his master and mistress home instantly.

On his quitting the room, she sat down, unable to support herself, and looking so miserably ill that it was impossible for Darcy to leave her, or to refrain from saying, in a tone of gentleness and commiseration, "Let me call your maid. Is there nothing you could take, to give you present relief? A glass of wine; shall I get you one? You are very ill."

"No, I thank you," she replied, endeavoring to recover herself. "There is nothing the matter with me. I am quite well. I am only distressed by some dreadful news which I have just received from Longbourn."

She burst into tears as she alluded to it, and for a few minutes could not speak another word. Darcy, in wretched suspense, could only say something indistinctly of his concern, and observe her in compassionate silence. At length, she spoke again. "I have just had a letter from Jane, with such dreadful news. It cannot be concealed from anyone. My youngest sister has left all her friends— has eloped—has thrown herself into the power of—of Mr. Wickham. They are gone off together from Brighton. You know him too well to doubt the rest. She has no money, no connections, nothing that can tempt him to— she is lost forever."

Darcy was fixed in astonishment. "When I consider," she added, in a yet more agitated voice, "that I might have prevented it! I who knew what he was. Had I but explained some part of it only—some part of what I learned—to my own family! Had his character been known, this could not have happened. But it is all, all too late now."

"I am grieved, indeed," cried Darcy, "grieved—shocked. But is it certain, absolutely certain?"

"Oh yes!—They left Brighton together on Sunday night, and were traced almost to London, but not beyond; they are certainly not gone to Scotland."

"And what has been done, what has been attempted, to recover her?"

"My father is gone to London, and Jane has written to beg my uncle's immediate assistance, and we shall be off, I hope, in half an hour. But nothing can be done; I know very well that nothing can be done. How is such a man to be worked on? How are they even to be discovered? I have not the smallest hope. It is every way horrible! When my eyes were opened to Wickham's real character—Oh! Had I known what I ought, what I dared, to do! But I knew not—I was afraid of doing too much. Wretched, wretched mistake!"

Darcy made no answer. He seemed scarcely to hear her, and was walking up and down the room in earnest meditation; his brow contracted, his air gloomy. Elizabeth soon observed and instantly understood it. Her power was sinking; everything must sink under such a proof of family weakness, such an assurance of the deepest disgrace. She should neither wonder nor condemn, but the belief of his self-conquest brought nothing consolatory to her bosom, afforded no palliation of her distress. It was, on the contrary, exactly calculated to make her understand her own wishes; and never had she so honestly felt that she could have loved him, as now, when all love must be vain.

But self, though it would intrude, could not engross her. Lydia—the humiliation, the misery, she was bringing on them all—soon swallowed up every private care; and covering her face with her handkerchief, Elizabeth was soon lost to everything else; and, after a pause of several minutes, was only recalled to a sense of her situation by the voice of her companion, who, in a manner, which though it spoke compassion, spoke likewise restraint, said, "I am afraid you have been long desiring my absence, nor have I anything to plead in excuse of my stay, but real, though unavailing, concern. Would to heaven that anything could be either said or done on my part, that might offer consolation to such distress!— But I will not torment you with vain wishes, which may seem purposely to ask for your thanks. This unfortunate affair will, I fear, prevent my sister's having the pleasure of seeing you at Pemberley today."

"Oh, yes. Be so kind as to apologize for us to Miss Darcy. Say that urgent business calls us home immediately. Conceal the unhappy truth as long as it is possible—I know it cannot be long."

"Of course. You may be assured of my secrecy." Darcy paused, then added, "I shall trouble you no longer. Please give my compliments to Mr. and Mrs. Gardiner, and accept my best wishes for a happier conclusion to this affair than can presently be foreseen."

Elizabeth stood. "Thank you." How the situation had reversed itself since that afternoon in the Hunsford parsonage! Now she was the one desiring Darcy's good opinion and affections, while he was departing with a wish to sever the connection. She had lost him; she would never see him again. But before they parted, she knew she must tell him somehow that she recognized the error of the terrible accusations she had made that day in April. He had shown by his gentlemanly behavior he had attended to her rebukes; she needed to demonstrate to him that she recognized her former opinions were based on lies and prejudice.

Gathering a desperate resolve, she said, "I would also like to thank you, sir, on my own behalf as well as that of my aunt and uncle, for the courtesy and hospitality you have shown us here. You and Miss Darcy have been all that is kind and amiable. Your sister is a charming and pleasant young lady, and I am very glad to have made her acquaintance, however briefly. Please know that, despite this unfortunate ending, these days in Lambton are ones I will always remember with pleasure."

For a moment his face remained closed and distant, almost pained, then he approached her. Somehow she found her hand in his, unsure who had initiated the contact.

She saw his mouth form the word "Elizabeth," though no sound emerged. Then, recalling himself, he took a deep breath and said formally, "Miss Bennet, the pleasure has been entirely mine." He paused, appearing to struggle for words for a moment, then added slowly, "I hope your acquaintance with Georgiana need not be brief. She has told me repeatedly of the pleasure she has had in your company, and I am certain that she will be most disappointed your stay is to be interrupted. She does not make friends easily, and is often lonely, I believe, for the company of other young women. May I hope, or do I ask too much, that you will continue the acquaintance, and perhaps correspond with her from time to time?"

The surprise of this application was great. She felt relief that, despite Lydia's shame, he would still at least consider her an acceptable companion for his sister. Then she realized all of his behavior—his closeness to her, his hand around hers, and most importantly that look in his eyes she was now coming to recognize—combined to tell her that though his words were about Georgiana, his meaning was quite different. In all respectability, he could not, as a single man, contact her directly, but Miss Darcy could; he was offering her a way to continue their own contact by proxy.

How had it come to pass that his good opinion was so important to her that this reassurance could bring tears once again to her eyes? Elizabeth struggled to calm herself. "I… I should like that, sir, very much."

The slightest of smiles warmed his face becomingly. "And perhaps, in happier times, you might honor us… honor her with a visit?"

To know he hoped to see her again, desired to see her enough to invite her to Pemberley! It seemed too much, coming so soon after despairing of any possibility of his favor. "Mr. Darcy," she said, then paused, gaining strength somehow from his steady gaze, "the honor would be mine, and I would delight in seeing Miss Darcy once again."

She would not have thought his gaze could become more intense. The sensations she felt as he raised her hand to his lips were such as she had never felt before, and the intensity of those feelings was so great she felt the need to drop her eyes, recalling she was alone with him and that in the tension of the moment neither he nor she might be best able to follow the dictates of appropriate behavior.

With that thought came the recollection of Lydia's situation—how could she have forgotten it even for a moment, and how could she so have forgotten herself as to be consenting to accept Mr. Darcy's addresses in light of Lydia's ruin? Her breath caught as tears began once again to overtake her, but even in her distress she felt the more than common awkwardness and anxiety of his situation, and she found herself tightening her fingers on his lest he perceive her loss of composure as a rejection of him.

"Miss Bennet, I must apologize for putting my… concerns before you at a moment when you are facing such distress," he said quietly, displaying an extraordinary sensitivity to her shift of mood. "Please, you must sit. You are not well." Releasing her hand most reluctantly, he led her to a chair.

Burying her face in her handkerchief, she whispered, "I am sorry."

"No, your feelings do you credit," replied Mr. Darcy. Had she been able to encounter his eyes, she might have seen how he was struggling not to take her in his arms to offer her whatever comfort he could. "But how may I be of assistance to you? You are eager to away to Longbourn; shall I ask your maid to pack your bags?"

She nodded, still unable to look up. He quitted the room, and she heard him call to the servant. When he returned, he slipped quietly into the chair opposite her.

"Miss Bennet, will you allow me to sit with you until your aunt and uncle return? There is no need for you to make conversation, but I do not wish to leave you alone at a time like this."

"As you wish, sir." Elizabeth tried to breathe deeply and calmly. Mr. Darcy handed her his handkerchief while taking her own damp one. Somehow in the process he managed to reclaim her hand with his.

Elizabeth's thoughts could not stay still. They fluttered from Lydia's disgrace to Mr. Darcy to the shame her family would face in the future. How hopeless it seemed that there could be any resolution to this crisis! She felt both pity and furious anger at Lydia for the thoughtless behavior that would ruin so many of the family's hopes, and then, with a sinking heart, connected those unhappy thoughts once again with the man next to her. Would she risk the reputation of the Darcy family name merely by association with them? She could not bear the idea she might do him harm, no matter how high the cost of preventing it. If that cost was never to see him again, she would pay it.

"Mr. Darcy," she said, her voice trembling, "I find I must ask you to reconsider your... willingness to further my acquaintance with your sister. It is certain that in light of this event my family's reputation will be severely harmed, and

I would anticipate many good families of much lower standing than yours will no longer consent to receive us. Will you risk associating your sister with a family in such disgrace?"

"Miss Bennet, what has your sister done that my sister would not have done were it not for an accident of timing? Surely there are no two people more likely to understand your position than Georgiana and I."

She could hardly believe her ears. Even with the many changes he had wrought in his behavior since Rosings, could he possibly be putting aside his pride so far as to compare Georgiana with Lydia?

"But in this case what *you* understand and what *society* understands are two very different matters. And I must argue with you, sir, in your comparison; though there are similarities in their situations, Miss Darcy is far more sensible than my heedless, thoughtless sister."

"They both took the same risk," he said with a dark look. "Miss Bennet, if you are attempting to tell me that you have for your own reasons changed your mind from the preferences you stated earlier, please tell me so at once, and I shall trouble you no more. But do not use your family as an excuse."

"You confuse my meaning entirely, Mr. Darcy; my feelings have not changed, but I am concerned about the wisdom of this course. Or perhaps," she said, hoping to inject a note of playfulness into the discussion, which seemed to be headed to dangerous ground, "I should say that my feelings have not changed *recently*, as we both have reason to believe my opinions not to be completely immutable."

"So long as you see no reason to change your opinions further, I see no reason for complaint."

The warmth of his gaze brought blushes to her cheeks and tremulous sensations new to her. She could not look away, and she longed to find a witty comment to lighten the atmosphere, but found all words failed her just as she needed them most.

He seemed as much caught as she, his fingers lightly stroking the back of her captive hand. Elizabeth felt hypnotized by the soft tracery of his touch, and was quite taken aback when he abruptly released her hand and pulled away, the old cold and distant look returning to his face.

She looked away, confused, wondering what had happened. Could she not manage to stay in accord with him for the length of a conversation? Or was she somehow misinterpreting him, as she had done so often in the past? She resolved that this time, at least, she would find a way to ask him, rather than assume, what he meant by his behavior.

Taking a deep breath, she said impertinently, "Pray, sir, what brings on the dread Darcy look of disapproval?"

"The dread Darcy look of disapproval?" he replied with a raised eyebrow and the slightest of smiles.

Elizabeth nodded gravely. "What sin could I have committed, I wonder? Could it have been something I said? Something I did? Hmmm—might you have taken a dislike to the style of my hair, or perhaps the color of my dress?"

Darcy could not help smiling, pleased to see her teasing him again. "As you know full well, Miss Bennet, I approve very much of everything about you. In fact, sometimes I approve far too much, and must then disapprove, not of you, but of myself."

"Disapprove of yourself! For approving of me? Come, sir, that is hardly friendly."

"Exactly my point, Miss Bennet."

"So approval leads to unfriendliness! I must assume I am supposed to ask how this could be, but I shall not fall into your trap, sir."

It has been too long since I have crossed wits with Elizabeth, Darcy thought, *but I must take great care on this point.* He said lightly, "I shall decipher the riddle for you anyway. I have always prided myself on my self-control, which has served me well until now. Since meeting you, however, I have discovered the sad truth—that my self-control is far more limited than ever I thought, though fortunately this difficulty seems to be limited to the times when I am in your most *approved* presence. I am sure you will appreciate my difficulty. Given how far my self-control eroded when you still disliked me, imagine how much more difficult it is to maintain in the presence of your smiles. Hence, I must disapprove of too much approval, lest it lead me to dangerous ground."

Dangerous ground, indeed, thought Elizabeth. "Mr. Darcy, I have every faith in your gentlemanly behavior."

He winced. She could not know how much he had been hurt by her words in Hunsford about his ungentlemanly behavior, so he tried to keep any bitterness out of his voice as he acknowledged the unhealed wound. "But as you yourself have pointed out in the past, I am quite capable of behaving in an ungentlemanlike manner."

"Pray, sir, do not remind me of the unjust and misinformed things I have said in the past! In cases such as these, a good memory is unpardonable."

"That particular reproof was well-deserved, as I recall."

Elizabeth flushed. "My philosophy is to think only of the past as it gives me pleasure, so I prefer instead to think about my current better understanding of you, which includes acknowledging that your behavior is gentlemanly in every way! But I shall try to heed your warning and not test your self-control, lest you be irreparably harmed by discovering its limits."

"Miss Bennet, I urge you to take care," he said intently, teasing put aside. "The only thing that separates me from this"—here he touched her letters—"is that self-control you mock. There is otherwise no difference between Mr. Wickham and me."

"Do not," she cried, "do not ever let me hear you comparing yourself in any way to that... that scoundrel! There is a world of difference between you!"

He smiled slightly. "Perhaps I should learn to criticize myself more often, for the pleasure of hearing you defend me."

WHAT WOULD MR. DARCY DO?

"I speak only the truth, and you, sir, know enough of my *frankness* to believe that!"

"Elizabeth, you are playing with fire. Trust *me* when I tell you not to trust me too far."

His use of her Christian name felt very intimate, and she sensed that some line had been crossed. She knew instinctively this was the moment when she should look away and change the subject, but instead she found herself saying, "And am I the only one playing with fire?"

"Touché," he said softly. "But do not say that I did not warn you." Taking her hand, he lifted her to her feet. "Elizabeth," he breathed as he slowly lowered his head and allowed his lips to caress hers for a brief moment.

Elizabeth felt the power of his touch run through her, shocked by both the sensation and her acquiescence—nay, her cooperation—in the kiss. What did it mean that she desired his kisses? Was he as shocked at her behavior as she was?

"Elizabeth,"—his voice made her name a caress—"Tell me to leave. Please." Even as he spoke, he pulled her closer and sought her mouth again, more urgently this time.

She allowed herself a moment of stolen pleasure, then, steeling her resolve, forced herself to say in the steadiest possible voice, "Mr. Darcy. You must stop, sir." She dropped her eyes, knowing instinctively she must not meet his gaze.

He inhaled sharply. "Yes, so I must." He firmed his resolve

and began to pull away, but could not resist the temptation to let his lips linger a moment on her hair as he did so.

Unfortunately, it was then and not a moment later that the door opened, revealing Mr. and Mrs. Gardiner.

Chapter 2

ELIZABETH AND DARCY HASTILY moved away from each other, but their faces told it all. There was a moment of shocked silence before Mrs. Gardiner, noting both Elizabeth's blushes and the tears returning to her eyes, hurried to her niece and took her aside, while a furious-looking Mr. Gardiner eyed Darcy.

Darcy exhaled through clenched teeth. Of all the situations to be caught in! What was he to say—*My apologies that I was taking advantage of your niece while she was too upset to stop me? Oh, and by the way, my father's godson has seduced your other niece and they have disappeared somewhere in London, and now you should trust me to help you find him?*

"Mr. Darcy," Mr. Gardiner said coldly, "Perhaps you will be so kind as to join me outside, as I have a few things to discuss with you." He held the door, motioning to Darcy.

Darcy gritted his teeth and followed, casting a worried

look at Elizabeth, who was now in tears in her aunt's arms—over Lydia rather than over him, he hoped. This was without question the most mortifying situation he had been in since—well, since the Hunsford parsonage, and he certainly had no one to blame but himself for this one.

Mr. Gardiner turned to face him. "Well, Mr. Darcy? I await an explanation of your behavior."

"Sir, I can offer no acceptable explanation," Darcy said stiffly. "My behavior obviously merits the severest of reproaches, and I stand prepared to take full responsibility for it."

"And do you often reduce young women to tears with your advances?" Elizabeth's distress clearly shocked Mr. Gardiner the most. After their visits to Pemberley it was evident to him that Darcy was very much in love with Elizabeth, which by itself had much inclined him in his favor, and all reports on him from his servants and the Lambton inhabitants indicated a man of strict honor. This behavior was incomprehensible to him.

"Sir, you misunderstand the situation. Her distress is unrelated to me. Miss Bennet will tell you she was already upset when I arrived. In fact it was my attempts to comfort her which turned into the cause for your concern. But Miss Bennet is indeed very upset regarding a separate matter, about which I must insist that you speak with her immediately."

"And I must insist, sir, on knowing your intentions toward my niece!"

Darcy ground his teeth. Clearly he would not be able

to raise Lydia's situation until he dealt with the infuriated Mr. Gardiner. "My intentions are completely honorable."

"Do I assume then you will accept my decision should I insist on taking steps to protect my niece's reputation?"

"Sir, I would marry her tomorrow if I could obtain her consent!" Darcy snapped, his temper fraying. "If you choose to insist on an immediate engagement, which is certainly within your rights, I would have neither reason nor desire to object, but I am afraid the same cannot be said for Miss Bennet!"

Mr. Gardiner blinked, surprised. "Do you have some reason to believe she would not consent to marry you?"

So Elizabeth had not told her family of his proposal! Little wonder that Mr. Gardiner was so furious! Darcy replied in a calmer but brittle voice, "I had assumed you were aware, sir, that she already refused me, not four months ago."

Mr. Gardiner, taken by surprise, but mollified by this knowledge, said, "That does cast a somewhat different light on things. But you say that she refused you—this hardly seems consistent with her behavior today. Are you certain you did not misinterpret her meaning?"

"Sir, I believe her exact words were that I was the last man in the world she could ever be prevailed upon to marry." Darcy felt a certain sense of bitter relief at finally unburdening himself of the words which haunted him constantly. "I defy any ability to misinterpret that."

Mr. Gardiner was taken aback. He could hardly credit that Lizzy would say anything of the sort, but, observing the pain in Darcy's eyes, he knew it to be true. He saw for a moment a very different Darcy, one who, underneath the image of the powerful scion of a wealthy family, was a young man who had received too much responsibility too soon, and who now found himself for the first time in the grips of a passion beyond his control. He softened considerably. "Well, young man, it would appear you have made a certain amount of progress since then, would it not?"

"There have been signs which might suggest warming of her regard toward me," Darcy cautiously allowed.

Mr. Gardiner chuckled. "Well, my boy, if what I saw in there was merely a suggestion of warming of her regard, I wonder what it would take to convince you that she actually liked you!"

"Sir, I... I appreciate your concern, and again, I will accept whatever consequences you choose to place on my actions."

"Well, Mr. Darcy, I will give this due consideration, but, while I cannot condone your behavior in any way, I am willing to accept that you did not intend to take advantage of Elizabeth. But it seems that I must consult with my niece at this point."

"I strongly urge you to do so, sir, as Miss Bennet has something she must discuss with you that cannot be delayed."

Mr. Gardiner, finding himself intrigued with this less controlled side of Mr. Darcy, suggested, "She seemed somewhat upset—perhaps in this case you should tell me this important news to spare her nerves."

"I doubt that I am the best person to tell you," Darcy demurred, but then, in response to a firm look from Mr. Gardiner, proceeded to unfold the details of the situation of the unfortunate Lydia, and the efforts being made to recover her. Mr. Gardiner's shock and dismay were as great as was to be expected, and he agreed that their departure was called for as soon as the current situation could be resolved.

Elizabeth, in the meantime, was far more preoccupied with her concerns over Lydia than her aunt's concerns over her improper behavior. "Aunt, I know that I should not have permitted it; it was a momentary weakness. Fortunately, we were not observed by anyone but you, and I see no reason to go any further with this when we have a true crisis to which we must respond!" she said with some vexation.

"Lizzy, my dear, you do not *believe* you were observed, but you have no way of knowing who might have passed by that window and looked in. Mr. Darcy is well known here, and his presence attracts a substantial amount of interest, and it is already known that you spent a significant amount of time closeted alone with him! I must take this seriously, even if you will not. Now, you tell me that you are not angry or upset with Mr. Darcy, and you clearly respond favorably to him in many ways, and it has been quite obvious to me since our arrival that he is very much taken with you. So I fail to see where the difficulty lies in taking the appropriate steps!"

Elizabeth closed her eyes and said slowly and very distinctly, "Because I am not yet ready to make a decision about him!"

"It seems to me that you already did make a decision, given what I saw, my dear," Mrs. Gardiner replied gently.

"I confess that I have been giving the matter of Mr. Darcy a good deal of thought these last few days, and I am generally favorably inclined at present, but I can go no further than that while Lydia's fate lies in question! Please, aunt, let this take its own course!"

"I do not know we have that option, Lizzy, especially under these circumstances, given that your family is already facing disgrace over Lydia's behavior."

Elizabeth turned sharply away and stared out the window. "And I have no desire to force that disgrace on Mr. Darcy, especially since it involves Mr. Wickham!"

A knock came at the door, and Mr. Gardiner entered. He observed Elizabeth's flushed cheeks, and quietly requested that his wife join him for a short discussion.

Elizabeth paced the narrow confines of the room. How could she have allowed this situation to arise? Was she now to be faced by the prospect of a forced engagement? Even as she fought against the idea, a part of her wondered if it would not be the simplest way out of her larger dilemma with Mr. Darcy. She knew that she respected and esteemed him; she felt gratitude to him, not merely for having loved her, but for loving her still well enough, to forgive all the petulance and acrimony of her manners in rejecting him. When she had thought earlier that she had lost any chance of his favor, she had felt the deepest of distress. His smiles brought her pleasure, and his touch… she shivered as she remembered the feeling of his lips on hers, and how she had felt the shock of it run through her.

Yet how could she base her future on these things, when in truth they had had no more than half a dozen completely civil conversations in the entirety of their acquaintance? And then there was the question of Wickham, and all that it implied. No, she simply could not agree, even if her heart traitorously wanted her to accept.

Two doors away, Darcy was sprawled in a chair, his agitation clear in his drumming fingers, wondering frantically what Elizabeth was thinking. Was she having warm thoughts of him—could she in fact have changed her mind about marrying him—or was she furious with him for putting her in this position? Would she ever forgive him if she were forced to marry him? He felt like a prisoner awaiting his sentence, and he was almost relieved when Mr. Gardiner entered the room and sat across from him.

"Well, I have spoken with my wife, and had a few minutes of private discourse with my niece. Fortunately for you, Elizabeth concurs with your story in all its particulars with the exception of one item,"—here his eyes twinkled for a moment—"which is that while you claim this affair is entirely your responsibility, my niece claims in fact it was she who provoked you. But I am prepared to overlook this discrepancy. However, the thornier question of what to do remains. Although Lizzy admits to being quite favorably disposed toward you at present, it appears that you were correct in your assessment that she is not prepared to enter of her own free will into an engagement at this point."

Darcy felt the sharp thrust of disappointment lance through him. So her warmth was only for the moment, and her feelings toward him had not changed.

Mr. Gardiner eyed him sympathetically. "If I, acting for her father, insist on it, she will not refuse to participate in an engagement, but I have some concerns about this idea. Lizzy has never been one to accept being coerced gracefully, and I fear that it would mean a very rocky start to any marriage between you. I would nonetheless insist on it, if it were not for the fact that both Mrs. Gardiner and I believe that in fact Lizzy is quite close to being ready to accept you, and perhaps it is even now only her distress over her sister that prevents us from resolving this to everyone's satisfaction.

"Here, then," he continued, "is my proposition: that, in the interest of your future marital harmony, we allow you a period of time to attempt to convince Elizabeth to accept you of her own accord, but if this meets no success in a few months, I will speak with her father regarding her participation. What do say you to this plan?"

The blistering pain of disappointment was still foremost in Darcy's mind. "I accept," he said shortly.

"Mr. Darcy," Mr. Gardiner said with some compassion,

"let me remind you that I would not have proposed this plan if I were not convinced in my own mind that Lizzy's consent will be yours in a very short time. Perhaps we should consider ways to offer you the opportunity to court her—for example, if you will be in town, we could invite her to stay with us at Gracechurch Street."

"As it happens, I have some plans for the next few weeks which may interfere with that, but are of concern to you, sir," Darcy said, and proceeded to outline to Mr. Gardiner his plans for discovering Wickham and Lydia in London, which led to much vigorous discussion and planning.

During the hurry and confusion of the next hour, Elizabeth was fortunately kept distracted by the business entailed by their rapid departure. There were notes to be written to all their friends in Lambton, with false excuses for their sudden departure, packing to be completed, and accounts to be settled. Had she been at leisure to be idle, she would have been in an agony of uncertainty over what Mr. Darcy could be thinking of her. Her uncle had not been at all forthcoming about his discussion with him, and she could only imagine what a man of such pride would feel about the situation in which they had been caught. So she was glad to have employment to keep her thoughts at bay.

Darcy, meanwhile, awaited his opportunity to bid farewell to Elizabeth with some trepidation. He felt unsure of his reception at a time when he most needed reassurance of her affection. He tried to remind himself he had the assurance of Mr. Gardiner that Elizabeth would be prevailed upon to marry him even if he could not win her, but the taste of that possibility was bitter.

When Elizabeth finally entered, he wanted nothing so much as to fling himself on his knees before her and beg her to marry him. Her loveliness took his breath away.

"Sir, you wished to speak with me?" she said after a moment, her eyes downcast.

He cursed himself. Here was his opportunity to make amends, and all he could think of was what her lips had felt like under his. "Yes, Miss Bennet," he said with a bow, "please accept my deepest apologies for my most inappropriate behavior earlier."

She looked up, fearing to see displeasure in his eyes, but finding none. "Your apology is accepted, Mr. Darcy, although, as I told my aunt, I believe you may have had some provocation." Was there just a hint of impudence in her voice? "I shall endeavor to remember in the future that your warnings should be taken with the utmost seriousness."

Darcy breathed a sigh of relief. Perhaps it was not so hopeless after all. "I hope I have not caused you undue difficulty with your family."

"Nothing that will not pass. I am trying to appreciate the novelty of being in trouble for misbehavior of this sort," she said in an attempt at lightness. Then, seeing the concerned look on his face, she clarified, "Truly, my aunt was quite gentle with me. And I hope my uncle was not overly harsh with you?"

Darcy gave a slight, ironic smile. "There were a few rough moments, but we eventually came to an understanding of sorts. The subject arose of my proposal in Kent, which helped to establish my bona fides, but I apologize to you, as it was something you clearly preferred to keep private."

"I... actually, it is probably just as well that they know, and I certainly would not want them to have... the wrong impression of you. The Gardiners' good opinion is important to me," she said, struggling for the right words.

"And *your* good opinion is important to *me*," Darcy replied, gazing intently at Elizabeth. "I hope I have not harmed that today."

"Sir, I..." Elizabeth stopped. Why could she not complete a thought in a coherent manner when he looked at her like that? "Please understand that this is not a situation I have found myself in before, but... you need have no regrets."

Darcy's eyes kindled, and Elizabeth forgot to breathe. Just then they heard Mr. Gardiner's voice calling Elizabeth to the carriage. "It appears it is time for our adieus, Miss Bennet. Had we more time, there is much more I would wish to say. But, as it is"—he glanced out the door, and seeing no one there, he added softly—"be warned I made no promises to your uncle that it would never happen again."

"I shall keep that in mind, sir," said Elizabeth demurely. "However, as you know, I am not easy to intimidate."

Darcy's slow smile seemed to melt her bones. "I suppose that if you do not appear at the carriage very soon, they will probably come looking for you."

"I would imagine so, sir," she said, feeling breathless.

"But perhaps it is worth taking the chance."

"Perhaps so," murmured Elizabeth, shocked at her own daring. Closing her eyes, she felt the touch of his hand on her cheek, then his lips brushed hers just long enough for her to realize that she never wanted him to stop.

"Your carriage awaits, Miss Bennet," said Darcy huskily. Elizabeth, unable to trust her voice, turned and headed for the door. Darcy followed her to the street, then handed her into the carriage. After a glance at Mr. Gardiner, he raised her hand to his lips for a moment before releasing it.

"Good day, Mrs. Gardiner, Mr. Gardiner," he said. "Good day, Miss Bennet."

❦

"I have been thinking it over again, Elizabeth," said her uncle as they drove from the town, "and really, upon serious consideration, I am much more inclined than I was to judge this matter of Lydia as your eldest sister does. It appears to me so very unlikely, that any young man should form such a design against a girl who is by no means unprotected or friendless, and who was actually staying in his colonel's family, that I am strongly inclined to hope for the best. Could he expect that her friends would not step forward? Could he expect to be noticed again by the regiment, after such an affront to Colonel Forster? His temptation is not adequate to the risk."

"I wish I could believe it," said Elizabeth. "But I do believe him capable of every form of neglect. He has been profligate in every sense of the word. He is as false and deceitful as he is insinuating."

"Upon my word," said Mrs. Gardiner, "I am of your uncle's opinion. It is really too great a violation of decency, honor, and interest, for him to be guilty of it. I cannot think so very ill of Wickham. Can you, yourself, Lizzy, so wholly give him up, as to believe him capable of it?"

"I wish I could pretend that I do not believe him capable of it, but I know too much of him!"

"I do believe it is time, Lizzy, for you to tell everything you do know about this situation," her uncle said gravely. "It is clear there is a great deal you have kept from us, and it seems that we now need to know it."

Elizabeth flushed. "I know, and now it is obvious that I should have told the world, but at the time it seemed otherwise. Till I was in Kent, and saw so much of both Mr. Darcy and his cousin, Colonel Fitzwilliam, I was ignorant of the truth myself. And when I returned home, the regiment was to leave Meryton in a week's time. As that was the case, neither Jane, to whom I related the whole, nor I thought it necessary to make the knowledge public; for what use could it apparently be to anyone? That such a consequence as this should ensue, you may easily believe was far enough from my thoughts. And, to my shame, I knew it would not be to my advantage to reveal all that I knew, for then I should have had to say more than I liked about my sources of information, and I considered it unwise to apprise my family of my interactions with Mr. Darcy."

"And that is another piece that I need to ask you to relate," said her uncle. "I think you had better tell us the whole story of your Mr. Darcy."

Elizabeth would, in fact, much rather not have told this part, but she acknowledged her uncle's right to question her about it after the events of the day. "He is not *my* Mr. Darcy, uncle."

"I think he might disagree with you there," her uncle replied mildly. "But pray continue."

Elizabeth blushed furiously. Slowly, and not very fluently, she attempted to relate the events that had happened in Kent, skimming only over the worst of her verbal interchange with Mr. Darcy after his proposal. She did not want them to think ill of her for her bitter words, nor did she wish to alter their perception of Mr. Darcy from the pleasant gentleman he had been at Pemberley. She explained how she had gradually given up her former prejudices after reading his letter, and of her shock at seeing him in Derbyshire, as well as her present doubts about the wisdom of her continuing any acquaintance with him after Lydia's shame and the involvement of Wickham.

Mr. and Mrs. Gardiner exchanged glances. The distress

in their niece's voice clearly spoke of the struggle between her heart and her head on this subject. "Time will tell," said Mr. Gardiner. "But I would ask you to keep in mind that Mr. Darcy is a young man in a good deal of pain over his feelings about you."

"What did he say to you?" Elizabeth cried.

"I believe that should remain between him and me, Elizabeth. I only urge you to consider that, whether or not you return his affections, I believe that a certain degree of gentleness on your part would be in order."

Elizabeth made no reply to this, and in fact did not speak again for some time, and then only on a different subject. That she had injured Mr. Darcy with her harsh words she could easily believe, but to think about him in pain because of her hurt more than she cared to admit. And if the Gardiners noticed an occasional tear in her eye, they were wise enough to say nothing of it, but had they seen the handkerchief she clutched so tightly in her hand, they would have seen that the initials on it were not her own.

Chapter 3

THEY REACHED LONGBOURN BY dinnertime of the next day. Elizabeth was very glad to see Jane, who greeted them with alternating smiles and tears, and perhaps even gladder the long trip was over, for it had left her far too much time to dwell not only on the painful subject of Lydia, but on her recent meetings with Mr. Darcy, which caused such feelings that it was difficult to determine whether pleasure or pain bore the greatest share. Unaccustomed to struggling with such conflicting emotions, she was determined to keep her thoughts concealed, but all too often she had found the perceptive eyes of her aunt and uncle upon her, and she feared that they might be observing more of her struggle than she would choose.

Jane had no news from London to report, but was able to impart to them all the details of Lydia's flight and Mr. Bennet's plans for discovering her. Mrs. Bennet had secluded herself in her rooms with greatly shaken spirits.

In the afternoon, the two elder Miss Bennets were able to be for half an hour by themselves; and Elizabeth instantly availed herself of the opportunity of making many enquiries, which Jane was equally eager to satisfy. For her own part, however, she told very little of her travels and adventures, and nothing at all of Pemberley. Though she longed to unburden herself to her dearest Jane, she knew that it would only add to her sister's distress. That night, as she was preparing for bed, she held Darcy's handkerchief in her hand for a long while, thinking back on all her history with him. Then, with a firm resolve, she folded it and carefully tucked it away in the box which held his letter to her from Kent. I cannot allow myself to dwell on these thoughts, she told herself resolutely. Either I shall see him again someday or I shall not, and for now my family needs all my energy and affection.

The whole party was in hopes of a letter from Mr. Bennet the next morning, but the post came in without bringing a single line from him. His family knew him to be on all common occasions a most negligent and dilatory correspondent, but at such a time, they had hoped for exertion. They were forced to conclude that he had no pleasing intelligence to send, but even of that they would have been glad to be certain. Mr. Gardiner, having only waited for the post, set off for London, promising to write as soon as he knew anything.

Mrs. Bennet, to the relief of her daughters, continued to be in seclusion; Mrs. Gardiner was most valuable in taking turns sitting with her.

On the following afternoon, Elizabeth and her sisters were in the drawing room, working predominantly in silence, when the sound of hoofbeats in front of the house was heard. Kitty immediately rushed to the window—she was having difficulty enduring the restriction to home, and dearly wished to go to Meryton—and said loudly, "Now what is he doing here?"

"Who is it, Kitty?" asked Elizabeth.

"It's Mr. Bingley!" Kitty cried.

Jane dropped her sewing, the color draining from her face. "It cannot be!" But a moment later they heard his familiar voice greeting the servant at the door. Elizabeth quickly handed her sewing back to her, and by the time he was shown in, a semblance of calm had been restored.

"Why, Mr. Bingley, what a surprise! I thought you still at Pemberley!" Elizabeth greeted him as he was shown in, covering for Jane's confusion.

"I was indeed, Miss Bennet, but some urgent business called me to Netherfield, and here I am!" His eyes drifted immediately to Jane.

"You must have left Derbyshire soon after I did, then."

"Just a few days. I have only arrived here today."

Elizabeth risked a glance at Jane, whose face was still pale, but composed. What could it mean, that he had only just arrived and was already calling at Longbourn, without even the prerequisite call to Netherfield by Mr. Bennet? Surely it must be because of Jane!

"I hope that the business which brings you here is not an unhappy one, Mr. Bingley," Elizabeth said.

"Ah… Nothing serious, just some… matters of the estate. I… ah… have not truly had a chance to assess the situation yet. I have another task, you see—I was asked to deliver a letter to Miss Elizabeth Bennet, so I thought I had best call here as soon as possible." This excuse might have been more credible had he not been gazing at Jane the entire time he was speaking.

"A letter for me?" Elizabeth asked, looking far more calm than she felt regarding an unexpected letter from Pemberley so soon after her own departure.

"From Miss Darcy," said Bingley. "As soon as she heard I was departing for Hertfordshire, she at once decided she must write you." He handed Elizabeth an envelope.

Jane, still ignorant of Elizabeth's encounters in Derbyshire, shot her a strange look.

"How lovely. I thank you for the service, sir. You are far more prompt than the post, and more welcome," Elizabeth said. "But, since you have already come so far, will you not stop with us for a bit of refreshment?"

Bingley beamed. He looked at Jane, noticed the empty seat beside her, and it was decided.

Estate business indeed, Elizabeth thought. Why is he really here? Darcy must have said something to him after their meeting at the inn. Her cheeks flushed at the memory of those moments with Darcy. How shocked Jane would be if she knew! She turned the letter over in her hands, wondering at its contents.

It was fortunate that Jane had by now sufficiently recovered herself to be able to carry on the conversation with Mr. Bingley, since now it was Elizabeth's turn to be distracted. Mr. Bingley's smiles at Jane continued unabated until his departure, with many promises to meet again soon. As soon as he was gone, Elizabeth walked out to recover her spirits and to find privacy to read her letter.

Dear Miss Bennet,

I hope this letter finds you well, and I hope you do not mind my seizing the opportunity to write to you since Mr. Bingley is traveling to Hertfordshire. My brother had told me that I might write to you if I wished, but I was not sure of the direction, so Mr. Bingley is performing a very useful service!—I hope your sister is better, I was most concerned when my brother told me that she was ill and that you had to go home immediately.—We have been all astir here.—Immediately the day after you departed, Fitzwilliam received news from London and had to leave for there on an urgent basis. Then the very next day, Mr. Bingley announced that he had business that could not wait in Hertfordshire, and would be leaving on the following day, so our party is quite depleted!—I confess that I wondered briefly about this rash of urgent business, especially as I had not known Mr. Bingley to have received any word from Hertfordshire—but I must have been unaware of it. But I realized I had been foolish—had there been any conspiracy, I am sure it would have been my brother who would have gone to Hertfordshire, and Mr. Bingley to London!

This situation has led me to some concern, though, and I hoped I might beg your advice on it. I hesitate to ask Fitzwilliam, since he would worry so, but I know that you would be the one he would want me to consult in his absence. I am sure my brother would expect me to solve this on my own—but I lack confidence in my solutions. Here is my concern—as you may know, my companion, Mrs. Annesley, has taken leave to visit her family during my stay at Pemberley, since I was to be with Fitzwilliam, but then of course he left, but Mr. Bingley is such a dear friend of his, and one I have known for years, that I felt all would be well. Now that he is leaving as well, but his family show no inclination toward going with him, nor returning to London, I have concern about being left the hostess here for Mr. and Mrs. Hurst and Miss Bingley.—It is, of course, quite improper for me to entertain anyone since I am not out.—I know you will respect my confidence when I tell you that Miss Bingley makes me most uncertain of myself. She asks so many questions of me, and I sometimes do not know how to answer, especially when her questions are about Fitzwilliam—and I know that she asks the servants as well. And Mr. Hurst's acquaintance with drink is something I do not know how to handle—how am I to behave?—But I also do not feel that I can ask them to leave. My brother said that he did not know when he would return, but that it might be several weeks. So any advice on what I should do would be most greatly appreciated!

I must tell you how very much I enjoyed meeting you. You are everything Fitzwilliam led me to expect, and I look forward to having the chance to get to know you much better.—Please do write soon.

Yours, etc.
Georgiana Darcy

It was well that Elizabeth had formed no expectations of the letter, as its contents were quite unforeseen, and excited a contrariety of emotions. That Bingley had no true business at Netherfield was hardly a surprise, though she was glad to have it confirmed. But it was clear Miss Darcy thought her relationship to Mr. Darcy was much closer than it in fact was. What had her brother been telling her, that Miss Darcy would approach Elizabeth so much as a family member? And had he spoken of her to his sister enough for her to have expectations, even before she came to Pemberley? Her thoughts whirled with all that Miss Darcy had let slip unknowingly.

It was then necessary to fend off the inquisitiveness of her family regarding her letter. She chose to say only that Miss

Darcy was a sweet girl, and that they had agreed to correspond after meeting briefly in Derbyshire, though this explanation drew questioning glances from Mrs. Gardiner.

Elizabeth's curiosity regarding Miss Darcy's concerns would not rest; she resolved to write back to her that very same day, and was able to send her response with the next post. She was not overly surprised, then, to receive another letter as soon as could be expected, only a day after her father's discouraged return from London.

Mr. Bennet took the occasion of the arrival of Georgiana's second letter to Elizabeth to tease her about her conquest of the Darcys. "Mr. Gardiner could not say enough good about Mr. Darcy while I was in London, though I certainly do not know what he could have seen in him. He went so far as to suggest that Mr. Darcy might be partial to you, Lizzy! But I assured him that he was imagining things, given your pointed dislike of the man and his perfect indifference to you."

Elizabeth, who was by this time tolerably well acquainted with her own feelings about Darcy, forced herself to smile. "Well, he does improve upon acquaintance. My uncle was no doubt struck by his condescension in allowing his sister to correspond with me."—among other things, she added to herself. She blessed Mr. Gardiner's discretion regarding the episode at the inn. She felt quite unready to discuss that with her family.

Miss Darcy's letter contained thanks for Elizabeth's good advice; Georgiana had, as advised, spoken with Mrs. Reynolds about finding a woman of good repute in Lambton to be her temporary companion, and was much relieved by this. She reported that Mr. Darcy remained in London, and that Miss Bingley grew daily more vexed with his absence. There were no references this time to Mr. Darcy holding Elizabeth in special regard, a fact which caused Elizabeth more distress than she cared to admit. She wrote back a cheery note—far more cheery than she felt, given the circumstances—detailing life at home with her sisters and the visits of Mr. Bingley and his obvious partiality to Jane—though Elizabeth cautioned her not to breathe a word of that to Miss Bingley.

The next day's post brought a letter from Mr. Gardiner with the happy news that Lydia and Wickham had been found, and that preparations were underway for their wedding. The relief this brought to the household was great. The violence of Mrs. Bennet's transports of joy was enough to make Elizabeth seek refuge in her own room, where she might think with freedom.

Although she rejoiced at Lydia's recovery from shame, Elizabeth found herself in an unusual lowness of spirits. Hard as it had been to bear the dread of Lydia's infamy, it was the more difficult when she thought of her last meeting with Darcy. The more she considered it, the more she saw in Lydia's elopement and marriage a probable end to her hopes. Although Darcy clearly had not given up all affection for her, Elizabeth's vanity was insufficient to believe that he could overcome, for a woman who had already refused him, a sentiment so natural as abhorrence against any relationship with

Wickham. Brother-in-law of Wickham! Every kind of pride must revolt from the connection. Even if he could tolerate it, how could he ever expose Georgiana to the possibility of Wickham as a relation? She could see no hope. As she began now to comprehend that he was exactly the man, who, in disposition and talents, would most suit her, she mourned that it was not to be.

She was distracted briefly from these thoughts when Jane confided to her in delight that Mr. Bingley had at long last proposed to her, and she attempted to rally her spirits lest Jane notice her state of mind. She would likely have been somewhat less than successful in this endeavor, had it not been for the fact that the household was all in an uproar with preparations for this new wedding with a date set for a little over two months hence, making it rather simple to disguise her feelings.

When the next letter from Miss Darcy arrived, Elizabeth found herself reluctant to open it at all. She found that she both longed to hear of Darcy, and feared it with the same thought. Any word of attachment on his part would bring up the pain of missing him; a word of indifference would be devastating.

> Dear Miss Bennet,
>
> What a pleasure to hear more about your family! How wonderful it must be to have so many sisters! Meryton sounds like a charming place.—I am glad to report that we are back to normal here since my brother returned

from London three days ago. I am so happy to have him home, not least because Miss Bingley does not pester me so much when he is here! He brought me home two lovely volumes of poetry which I am looking forward to reading. I gather that the business in London did not go well, since he must return in a fortnight, and he seems quite displeased with it, which is so unlike my dear brother.— He has promised me that the Hursts and Miss Bingley will not stay past his departure, which is a great relief, and he asks me to send you many thanks for your good advice. He seemed very pleased to hear I had been writing to you. I must admit I have found that I so enjoy the company of Mrs. Denniston, my new companion, that I think I shall beg Fitzwilliam to have her stay anyway, at least until Mrs. Annesley returns. I have been working on a new piece of music by Mozart which is very challenging, and she has been so encouraging when I am frustrated.—It now appears that I will be staying here at Pemberley until Christmas, which means I shall not have to miss any of the lovely autumn here. The Peaks are so beautiful in the autumn—I hope I can show them to you some day!—My brother asks me to send you his very best regards and his compliments to your family. I am sure he would prefer to deliver them in person!

Yours, etc.
Georgiana Darcy

Elizabeth wished she could be as certain as Miss Darcy. She wondered how much of Georgiana's enthusiasm for her brother's esteem of her arose from wishful thinking on her part rather than from anything he might have said, and these painful thoughts led to a tearful retreat to her room, where she found comfort in holding Darcy's handkerchief.

That night she decided to open her heart to Jane. She started by telling her about meeting Darcy at Pemberley, and their several meetings there. Jane was perhaps less surprised by parts of this than Elizabeth had anticipated, having already concluded from a variety of evidence that her sister was concealing a great deal.

"You never mentioned seeing Mr. Bingley on your journey, then, the day he first arrived back at Netherfield, you said that you had thought him still at Pemberley," said Jane. "And you never said anything about Miss Darcy either, and then she was suddenly a regular correspondent. I still owe all my information of your acquaintance with her to another source."

"There are parts of the story, though, that Mr. Bingley would not be able to relate to you, which will perhaps explain why I have been so reticent. But I must warn you, this will not reflect well on me, and you are likely to be shocked and disappointed."

Jane promptly reassured her dear Lizzy that nothing could change her high opinion of her, but she did prove to be somewhat shaken when Elizabeth told her of her encounter with Darcy after receiving the news of Lydia's elopement.

However, a moment's reflection allowed her to find a point of view which rendered near guiltless all of the people of whom she was so determined to think well. She earnestly explained to Elizabeth that clearly she had not been herself at the time, owing to the severe shock of Lydia's behavior; Mr. Darcy, of whom it was now a matter of anxiety to think well, was perhaps distressed beyond himself by the prospect of losing Elizabeth for a second time. Her poor aunt and uncle had no doubt been overwhelmed by the simultaneous problems of their two nieces.

Elizabeth had to laugh at this picture. "Dear Jane, you cannot have us all so clear of conscience, I am afraid. That Mr. Darcy and I were both in distress I will grant you, and it might possibly excuse our initial encounter, but the second must simply be put down to bad behavior on both of our parts. And I do not believe the Gardiners were overly distressed about the outcome; they came out of the entire episode thinking so highly of Mr. Darcy that they are now his greatest advocates."

"But Lizzy, how distressed you must have been about all of this! Whatever will you do when you see him again?"

"I believe that a wide range of options are possible. Being civil seems a possibility, though hiding or running away in a panic might be more appropriate. Or, if all else fails, I could always behave badly again."

An earnest entreaty to be serious had the desired effect, and the next hour was spent in conversation.

It did not take long for Elizabeth's natural high spirits to begin to reassert themselves after this event, and she soon seemed restored to her usual teasing, cheerful self. She was able to reply to Miss Darcy with a newsy account of Jane and Bingley's happiness. If sometimes she seemed to be taking longer walks than usual, or on occasion a shadow seemed to pass behind her eyes, no one but Jane seemed to notice. If from time to time she put her hand over her pocket where a particular handkerchief lay, no one could attach a meaning to it. By the time Georgiana's next letter arrived, Elizabeth felt prepared to read it with a tolerable degree of composure, if not necessarily the degree of inward calm she would prefer.

Dear Miss Bennet,

It is always a pleasure to hear from you, but I must admit the arrival of your letters is becoming quite a source of entertainment in itself. My brother thinks I do not notice how he watches for the post now, but how could I miss the way he hovers in an agony of suspense over me when I read your letters until I finally take pity on him and allow him to read for himself, and then he spends no less than half an hour admiring your letter, for it cannot possibly take him so long to read it! It is a shock to see Fitzwilliam act in such a distracted way, he is usually so dignified. If I had your courage, I should tease him about it, but as it is, I can only hope you do not keep him in suspense for too long, as I wonder how he will survive it!—I hope you do

*not mind my teasing you a little on this matter; you are far
less intimidating than my brother can be, and I must tease
someone!—I am so pleased for Mr. Bingley and your sister; Fitzwilliam says they have been in love for a long time
so I know they deserve all of their happiness. Of course we
shall be there for the wedding! I am so looking forward to
meeting your family, especially your sisters. I hope they will
like me! Please do tell me more about them; I feel that I am
getting to know them already!*

Yours etc.,
Georgiana Darcy

Elizabeth had to re-read this letter several times before
she could take in its contents. She could hardly believe Miss
Darcy's description of her brother, yet it was inconceivable
that the shy, quiet girl would invent such a story. It was
delightful to see Georgiana begin to express herself with more
confidence, but could it be true that Mr. Darcy still held so
active an interest in her, and made no effort to disguise it?
Her heart hammered at the thought.

She thought long and carefully before crafting her reply.

Dear Miss Darcy,

*I am impressed at the progress you are making in
your ability to tease if you can already even consider teasing your brother! But I will be happy to give you further*

instruction in how to proceed, since Mr. Darcy is certainly in need of a great deal of teasing. If your brother is again watching you as you read this, be sure to give an occasional gasp, and to say "Oh, no" from time to time, or perhaps "she couldn't possibly!" Then, when he asks you what is the matter, explain that you could not possibly tell him, since the letter is full of secrets that I have begged you to hold in confidence. Then, if he keeps asking, you may tell him that he may perhaps read the last few sentences, but only if he promises not to look at the rest of it. You may, of course, choose to elaborate on these ideas if you feel inspired!

Elizabeth continued the letter with news of the household, then impulsively added an invitation to Georgiana to visit at her home for a week or two before the wedding if she wished to discover what it was really like to have so many sisters.

She was very pleased with this letter, feeling it struck a delicate balance between acknowledging Georgiana's points without putting any overemphasis on Mr. Darcy's behavior.

Georgiana's reply came a few days later with an enthusiastic acceptance of the invitation to visit. For once, she barely mentioned her brother, which disappointed Elizabeth until she turned to the second page and saw, underneath Georgiana's signature, several lines written in a firm hand which she knew well from her many perusals of Mr. Darcy's letter to her at Hunsford. Her heart beating quickly, she jumped ahead to read the postscript:

> My *dear* Miss Bennet, I certainly hope you had as much enjoyment in crafting your last letter as my sister had in reading it, although I, as the proposed victim, must admit to a certain trepidation if you continue to encourage Georgiana in this manner. Thank you for making her laugh; she still does it too rarely. I look forward to seeing you again next month, even if you and Georgiana have had some days together in advance to plot my downfall—I shall attempt to face it with dignity. As ever, yours, FD

Chapter 4

MRS. BENNET, AFTER MANY searches, discussions, and nego-
tiations, finally decided that the gowns available in Meryton
could not possibly satisfy for a marriage to a man with five
thousand a year, and to this purpose she resolved to take Jane
to London to visit the dressmakers there. Elizabeth and Kitty
were to accompany them; Mary owned that she had rather
stay at home, as she had little interest in such frivolities.

Elizabeth was initially pleased to be taking the trip, feeling
it might provide her a useful distraction from her thoughts,
but after one agonizing day of making the rounds of the
dressmakers, she felt she could no longer tolerate the misery
of watching her mother's excitable behavior and Kitty's sulks,
even for Jane's sake. Hence, the following morning found
her pleading a sick headache and making plans to stay at
home with her aunt. Once the shopping party had departed,
however, Mrs. Gardiner was pleased to notice a substantial

improvement in her niece's health and was gratified to have Elizabeth to herself, since there was a certain subject she wished to broach with her.

"Lizzy, your uncle and I were wondering recently about your Mr. Darcy—do you know how old he was when his father died?"

Elizabeth, most startled by this application, found herself stammering, "I believe it was in the vicinity of five years ago, so he must have been twenty-two or twenty-three, I would imagine. But why do you ask?"

"No reason, my dear, except to settle the question between your uncle and me, but he has the right of it, then; I had thought it was more recent. It is your uncle's belief that much of Mr. Darcy's seriousness stems from having been left too young with all the responsibilities of managing a large estate, as well as raising a sister at a delicate age. I argued he has more of a capacity for liveliness than he might be credited for, but perhaps needs the right companion to help him find it."

"Aunt," said Elizabeth in some exasperation at this hinting, "why, pray tell, were you discussing Mr. Darcy in the first place?"

"Well, naturally, he does have an obvious interest for us, and also we saw a good deal of him when he was late in London."

"I have heard nothing of this," said Elizabeth carefully.

"Really? I would have supposed you to have sources of information… but no matter. Mr. Darcy called on us here shortly after my return from Longbourn, and afterward was our guest on several occasions. I must say that I have been very favorably impressed by him, and he and Mr. Gardiner seem to have established a fine regard for one another. I gather Mr. Darcy solicited his advice on more than one occasion regarding some difficulties he faces in managing a particular situation at Pemberley; thus, it would seem, confirming your uncle's opinion that his responsibilities are quite large for such a young man."

Elizabeth had not any idea of how to interpret this intelligence. Mr. Darcy seeking out advice from her uncle in trade? "You seem to take quite a lively interest in Mr. Darcy, aunt."

"And you do not? Come, my dear, he has made no secret to us of his hopes regarding you, unlike my sly Lizzy who will choose to keep everyone guessing! And when I hear from Jane that you have been somewhat out of spirits this last month, I must wonder what part he plays in that, as well."

Elizabeth sought to avoid her aunt's eyes as she pondered what she was willing to say. "I will not attempt to deny that he has been much in my thoughts, nor that I have moments when I wish he was near, but the situation is perhaps more complex than it seems at first glance. I know he does still hold me in some special regard, but he has by no means renewed his addresses, and there are certainly reasons to think he never will do so."

"Lizzy, how can you doubt it? He is clearly violently in love with you," said Mrs. Gardiner with a smile.

"Yes, and just as clearly, the person he detests most in the world, the man who disgusts him completely, is now my brother! I cannot believe that he would tolerate being in the same room as Wickham, much less become a relation of his!"

"I believe you seriously underestimate what he is willing to do for you, my dear."

"If I am so incorrect, why has he made no effort to see me?" Elizabeth said, finally admitting to the worry that was often with her. "He has traveled from Pemberley to London and back twice, and has never stopped in Hertfordshire, though with Mr. Bingley at Netherfield, nothing could be easier."

Mrs. Gardiner sighed. "Perhaps it is because he remains quite uncertain of your regard for him."

"How could he possibly be unsure of my regard after my behavior in Lambton?" asked Elizabeth in some exasperation.

"Lizzy, my dear, your regard for him is obvious to me, but do keep in mind, you have refused him twice, which would give anyone some cause for doubt."

"Not twice, only once, and that was long before Lambton!"

"And how would you portray your decision at Lambton? When we discovered you and strongly advocated to both of you that steps be taken to protect your honor, he was completely willing to enter into an engagement, and you categorically refused! Did you think that would have no effect on him?"

Elizabeth paled, deeply dismayed at her aunt's view of the affair. "I was not ready, but I never meant that as a refusal…

I never intended to hurt him in any way!" Tears rose to her eyes at the thought.

Mrs. Gardiner looked at her long and seriously. "My dear Lizzy, there are moments when I think that you and Mr. Darcy have a positive talent for misconstruing each other. I will speak openly to you: first, Mr. Darcy does indeed bear a significant burden of distress owing to his fear he will never win your affections, and second, if you think his dislike of Wickham is more powerful than his affection for you, then you are quite in the wrong. I do not wish to violate a confidence, but I will say that he has made it quite clear to me that he is willing to tolerate Mr. Wickham if need be for your sake."

Elizabeth, quite sobered by her aunt's statements, soon pleaded a return of her headache which required a retreat to her room, where she spent a great deal of time and tore up several sheets of paper before constructing a letter to suit her particular purposes.

Two days later, the post brought to Pemberley two letters, one to Mr. Darcy from Mr. Gardiner, the other to Miss Darcy from Miss Bennet. Darcy laid the first aside, and, caressing the second in his hand for some moments, decided it was time to practice some of his vaunted self-control, and rang for a footman to take it to Miss Georgiana. With a sigh, he broke the seal on Mr. Gardiner's letter.

Dear Mr. Darcy,

I have several thoughts which may apply to the situation regarding your tenant, but first, my wife bids me to send you her greetings, and to tell you that we are presently enjoying a short visit from my sister Bennet and her daughters. I am most particularly to tell you that while Miss Jane Bennet looks every bit the joyous bride, her sister Elizabeth appears to be somewhat out of spirits, the which, Mrs. Gardiner, having had extended discourse with her, tells me seems to be regarding the absence of a certain gentleman from Derbyshire. I cannot personally attest to any of this, since the young lady in question did not appear for dinner this evening, pleading a headache.

Now, regarding your tenant, it appears to me that you are faced with one of three choices…

Darcy stared at this surprising missive for several minutes. Bless Mrs. Gardiner! he thought. He felt overtaken by a desire to saddle the nearest horse and head posthaste to London, but he cautioned himself sternly that he must not make assumptions; he knew of the Gardiners' intentions for Elizabeth and him, and perhaps Mrs. Gardiner had taken an overoptimistic view of something Elizabeth had said.

Remember, man, you will see her for yourself in only a few weeks, he admonished himself. *Patience!*

His thoughts were interrupted by a gentle knocking on the

door. Georgiana entered tentatively in response to his call. "Fitzwilliam? May I speak to you for a moment?" she asked.

He attempted to calm himself. "Of course. What can I do for you?"

She looked at him oddly. "Is anything the matter?" she asked.

Of course! She had just received a letter from Elizabeth, and he was showing absolutely no interest in it. No wonder she was confused.

"No, nothing at all, Georgiana. What does Miss Bennet have to say today?"

Somewhat tentatively, she held out a folded sheet of paper. "She asked me to give you this."

He all but snatched it out of her hand. Georgiana smiled to see him returned to normal on the subject of Miss Bennet. "I will just go back to my letter, then?" she suggested timidly.

"Very tactful, dear," he responded with a laugh as she exited.

He was pleased to see that his hands barely trembled as he opened the letter.

Dear Mr. Darcy,

I hope you will forgive the impropriety of my address-ing this to you directly; it is a liberty I take out of con-cern for your sister on her upcoming visit to Longbourn. Sir, I regret having to raise an unpleasant matter, but, as you are perhaps aware, my youngest sister recently married and moved to the far north. While it is certain that neither she nor her husband will be in attendance in

Hertfordshire during the time of Miss Darcy's visit, it is likewise certain that her name will be raised repeatedly by members of my family, and I certainly would not wish Miss Darcy to be taken by surprise by mention of Mrs. Wickham. I defer to your greater authority as to whether it is best for you to discuss this with her in advance, or if it is something best addressed only when she arrives, in which case I will of course be prepared to handle the question in whatever way you see fit. Please consider yourself at liberty to share any information regarding my sister's situation that you deem appropriate.

Blast Wickham! Would he never stop haunting him? This was hardly what he hoped to hear from Elizabeth. He continued:

On a happier subject, I can safely say that Mr. Bingley and my sister are so deliriously happy as to be occasionally somewhat painful to those of us whose sources of such pleasure may be at a more distant remove. I remind myself that time will heal all these ills, but patience has never been one of my stronger virtues. Perhaps I should endeavor to follow your excellent example and make a study of the strengths and limitations of self-control, instead. Perchance you would be willing to offer me a review of the subject after your arrival at Netherfield?

Affectionately yours, EB

If Mr. Gardiner's letter had surprised him, Elizabeth's left him in a state of astonishment. He forced himself to peruse it several times, and even after he finally convinced himself he was reading it correctly, his amazement was such that he could not bring himself immediately to believe she had truly meant the words she had written. Whether his shock was greatest from Elizabeth's admission of missing him, her provocative flirtation, or the completely compromising adieu was impossible to determine.

As his astonishment began to fade, it was replaced by a sensation of heartfelt delight such as he had never felt before. Elizabeth wanted to see him! In his mind, he could picture her looking at him with that expression of warm welcome which she had worn so often for him in his dreams, but never in reality.

He read the letter once more, then folded it and placed it in his pocket next to a certain handkerchief. Decisively, he strode off in search of his valet, whom he informed of the immediate need to prepare for a brief trip. That accomplished, he searched out Georgiana in the music room, and informed her that business called him away for a few days.

Georgiana looked concerned for a moment, then gave a bright smile. "Please do say hello to your business for me when you see her," she said with an innocent look.

He gave her a look of mock sternness, but was in far too high spirits to argue the point with her.

As Bingley rode up to the paddock for his daily visit, Kitty, from her post in the window seat, announced, "There is a gentleman with him, mamma. Who can it be?"

"Some acquaintance or other, my dear, I suppose; I am sure I do not know."

"La!" replied Kitty, "It looks just like that man that used to be with him before. Mr. what's his name. That tall, proud man."

"Good gracious! Mr. Darcy!—and so it does I vow. Well, any friend of Mr. Bingley's will always be welcome here to be sure; but else I must say that I hate the very sight of him."

Jane looked at Elizabeth with surprise and concern. She knew how much her sister had been both longing for and dreading this encounter, and felt for the awkwardness that must attend Elizabeth, in seeing him for the first time since the events in Derbyshire.

The color which had been driven from Elizabeth's face by Kitty's announcement returned for half a minute with an additional glow, and a smile of delight added lustre to her eyes, as she thought for that space of time, that his affection and wishes must still be unshaken. But she would not be secure. There was too much that could have altered.

Her thoughts then flew to the letter she had written to him from Gracechurch Street. Would he have received it already? She frantically counted back the days since posting it, and deduced that it certainly could have arrived by this time, but of course he might well have left Pemberley before its arrival. She closed her eyes as she thought of the immod-est things she had written in it—what must he be thinking of her?

"Let me first see how he behaves," said she to herself. "It will then be early enough for expectation." She sat intently at work, striving to be composed, and without daring to lift up her eyes as the servant was approaching the door. On the gentlemen's appearing, she curtsied with her usual smile to Bingley, then turned to Darcy to find his serious gaze upon her. Immediately the memory of their last parting came into her mind, and an awareness of all that her family did not know; then, cognizant that she was blushing under his regard, she sat back down again to her work, with an eagerness which it did not often command. She ventured only one more glance at Darcy. He looked serious as usual; and she thought, more as he had been used to look in Hertfordshire, than as she had seen him at Pemberley. But perhaps he could not in her mother's presence be what he was before her uncle and aunt. It was a painful, but not an improbable, conjecture.

Darcy, fortunate in finding himself rapidly dismissed by Mrs. Bennet in favor of her civilities to Mr. Bingley, took the opportunity to sit in the chair nearest Elizabeth. As so often in the past, he was silent, seeming content merely to be near her. Elizabeth herself felt far from calm, and was perturbed by her acute awareness of his proximity.

"Have you come from Pemberley, Mr. Darcy?" asked Elizabeth, carefully watching her embroidery.

"Yes, I only arrived at Netherfield late yesterday."

"It is early yet for a hunting party."

"I did not come to go hunting."

Elizabeth glanced up and met his eyes. His intent gaze was on her; she had forgotten the danger of losing herself in those dark eyes. A slight smile touched the corners of his mouth, and her spirits fluttered in response. Forcibly collecting her thoughts, she said, "I am sure Mr. Bingley is most happy to have your company, especially since his visit to Pemberley earlier this summer was cut short."

"I am very happy to be here."

He has received the letter, she thought with agitation. Something had altered in his demeanor since they had last met, some sense, perhaps, of assurance. Aloud, she said, "I hope Miss Darcy was well when you saw her last."

"Quite well. She greatly enjoys your correspondence," he replied. "Your last letter was a particular favorite, I believe."

"I… am always glad to hear from her. I hope it will allow me to know her better; she seems less shy in her letters."

"Sometimes there are things that are easier to say in a letter than in person, I believe."

"I suspect you are correct, sir," she responded, her cheeks flushed.

The conversation lapsed, and they sat in silence for some minutes, listening to the cheerful discussion of wedding plans across the room.

"They seem very happy," Darcy commented.

"Yes, I believe they are. I suspect that we may owe thanks to you for Mr. Bingley's precipitous return to Netherfield."

"It was long overdue," he acknowledged.

Elizabeth wondered how anyone in the room could possibly be oblivious to the rising tension between the two of them. Her cheeks felt hot enough to make her long for a fan.

In some desperation, she said, "Mr. Darcy, would you care to view our gardens? They are particularly lovely at this time of year."

Darcy's smile grew deeper. "A delightful idea, Miss Bennet."

When Elizabeth told her mother of this intention, Mrs. Bennet pulled her aside into the hallway. "An excellent plan, Lizzy," she whispered. "That will keep him out of Mr. Bingley's way. I hope you will not mind it too much: it is all for Jane's sake, you know." Her daughter could not help feeling slightly amused by this interpretation.

Elizabeth was more than relieved to be leaving the stifling confines of the crowded drawing room. Stepping outside, she closed her eyes and drew in a deep breath of the fresh air. Feeling revitalized, she favored Darcy with an unrestrained smile.

Darcy's eyes warmed in response, and Elizabeth found her pulse quickening. As they began their progress across the lawn, Elizabeth found herself walking closer to Darcy than was strictly necessary. She was amazed that she could feel at the same time both so agitated and so content.

"Miss Bennet?"

"Yes, Mr. Darcy?" She smiled up at him.

"Would it be inappropriate for me to tell you how happy I was to receive your letter?"

Elizabeth, sensible of a certain fluttering inside her, raised an eyebrow. "I doubt it could be any more inappropriate than it was for me to write it in the first place," she said impertinently. "Perhaps I should be grateful you were not offended."

"Hardly, Miss Bennet. If that was offensive, please feel free to offend me at any time."

"Are you encouraging me, sir?" she asked with mock disapproval.

"Very much so." His gaze turned serious. "I have missed you, Elizabeth," he said softly, speaking her name as if it were the most intimate of endearments.

Elizabeth felt an array of sharp sensations course through her. She felt unable to respond, or perhaps more truly that should she attempt to respond, she might say too much, so she limited herself to drawing closer to his side and taking his arm. Though the contact gave her a surge of pleasure, she almost immediately doubted her wisdom in initiating it; she had forgotten the power his touch had on her, and she shivered as she felt his breath in her hair.

"You are perfectly safe, Miss Bennet. We are in full view of the house," he said, misinterpreting her reaction.

"I appreciate your reassurance, sir, but I assure you that I do not feel unsafe."

He put his free hand lightly over hers. "I am glad to know

that you recognize that I do still have some self-control where you are concerned."

"Are we returning to the question of self-control, then, sir?" She looked up at him teasingly.

"Miss Bennet, I will happily discourse on any subject matter of your choice, but perhaps it would be wiser to focus on patience rather than self-control."

Elizabeth felt it safest to change the subject. "I understand that you had the opportunity to see my uncle and aunt Gardiner when you were late in London."

He gave her a questioning look. "I did indeed have the pleasure of calling on them," he said somewhat cautiously.

"So my aunt told me when I spent several days with them last week." She added playfully, "It would appear that you have obtained quite an advocate in Mr. Gardiner. He could not praise you enough to my father when he was in London."

"I am honored," said Darcy, "especially as I suspect my reputation with your family can benefit from any advocacy that is available. I assume from my reception earlier that your parents are still unaware of our... more recent encounters?"

"I assure you that you could not possibly have got away from my mother with the ease you did had she the slightest idea!"

"Nor, I expect, would I have been allowed to walk out with you alone."

Elizabeth blushed. "Fortunately, the Gardiners have been most tactful in that regard, and settle for singing your praises at any opportunity. I have limited myself to noting that you improve upon further acquaintance," she said playfully, glancing up at him through her lashes with a look of mock seriousness.

"I hope to have sufficient further acquaintance in which to continue to improve, then, Miss Bennet."

"Will you be remaining at Netherfield until the wedding, Mr. Darcy?"

"No, unfortunately I can stay but two days, as I must return to Pemberley quite shortly owing to a situation there that requires my personal intervention."

Elizabeth, startled by the depth of disappointment she felt, said, "I am surprised you would make such a long journey for such a short stay."

"Surely, Miss Bennet, you must have known when you wrote to me, that I would not be able to stay away," he said softly.

Elizabeth cast her eyes down in embarrassment. "No, sir, in fact I did not know that."

"You are less than certain of me? You need not be."

"It is difficult to be certain of anything at times such as these."

"Elizabeth, you know what my hopes and wishes are."

"Mr. Darcy," she responded slowly, struggling to find the words and the courage to express herself, "while you may rest assured that I receive your words with gratitude and pleasure, please understand that there have been a great many changes in my life of late, sir, not the least of which concern you. A month ago I had every expectation of my four sisters remaining at home with me for some time; now, I face living apart from my dearest Jane for the first time, and I do not expect to see my youngest sister again beyond the briefest of visits. Many things in my family will not be the same again, and I include myself in that. That same month ago I fully expected never to see you again, sir, and certainly in no way could I have foreseen the changes that would occur in a bare three days in Lambton. I have done things I would never have imagined, and I have learned that I did not know myself so well as I had thought." She paused, and risked a glance at Darcy.

He looked thoughtful. "And time is needed to accept these changes before facing any others?"

Elizabeth nodded silently.

"I can be patient, if I know I have reason to hope."

She found herself longing for his touch, and fought her body's treacherous urges. She forced herself to say, "And there is another, less pleasant matter which must be faced."

"And that is?"

"To my regret, I am forced to call brother a man whose name you rightfully must wish never to hear again."

Darcy stopped and turned to face her. With determination, he said slowly, "I will not attempt to conceal that I would wish never to hear of or see George Wickham again, but please understand me clearly, Miss Bennet, I will not allow him to come between you and me. I will not let him cost me what is dearest to me ever again. And if this requires that I acknowledge his existence upon occasion, so be it."

Relief coursed through her. "I will endeavor to remember that."

"Thank you."

Elizabeth, feeling overwhelmed by the import of their conversation, ran her fingers through the flowers as she passed. She paused for a moment, then broke off a sprig of flowers, allowing the sweet scent to soothe her restless spirits. He raised an eyebrow. "Lavender, Mr. Darcy. It is a favorite of mine."

"An unusual favorite—I believe most ladies would choose the rose," Darcy said, and Elizabeth felt gratitude that he had so well understood her need to move to a more neutral issue.

"Perhaps what pleases me is different. Lavender is not so bright or showy as roses are, but it is hardier and smells as sweet."

"If we are to be choosing flowers for their virtues, perhaps I should give you forget-me-nots."

"Then we both favor the flowers of the springtime, for I would have to choose sweet williams for you," she said daringly.

Their eyes caught and held. Elizabeth found her breath coming quickly. Darcy reached out a hand and touched the inside of her wrist. "Miss Bennet, I have said I can be patient if I have hope. Can you give me that?"

Blushing, she said, "I believe you already know the answer to that, Mr. Darcy."

"Some answers need to be heard."

Elizabeth felt dizzy. "Sir, if I were to follow only the dictates of my heart, you may rest assured that you would be satisfied."

The power of his gaze as he gripped her hand tightly was irresistible. He reached out to touch her face, and she became achingly conscious of how little she wished to resist him. Carefully, she looked away, and taking his arm once again, directed them to begin walking again. Lightly, she said, "I would remind you, sir, that we still remain in full view of the house."

"But it would be difficult for an observer to see in detail at this distance," he said, allowing his lips to caress her hair lightly. Placing a finger under her chin, he tipped her face gently up until their eyes met again. "And no one will hear if you call me by my name."

She could not resist him. Her longing was evident in her voice as she whispered, "Fitzwilliam." His eyes blazed, and, as if hypnotized, she watched his face lowering toward hers until she could resist the pull no longer, and raised her lips to his.

Somehow Darcy found the strength to pull back after the briefest taste of the pleasure of her kiss. "Dearest, loveliest Elizabeth," he murmured.

Because she could not stop herself, she raised a hand and touched the tips of her fingers to his cheek. The feeling of his skin seemed to burn down her arm, and her face unconsciously reflected the yearning she felt. Darcy closed his eyes against the invitation he read in her eyes, and, taking her hand from his cheek, he kissed her palm, her fingers, the soft skin inside her wrist. He heard the sharp intake of her breath, and felt the last of his control beginning to dissolve. "Elizabeth," he said urgently, "we must not…" But even as he spoke, he was drawing her into his arms and seeking her mouth with ever-increasing urgency.

Elizabeth's astonishment in the pleasure of his kisses paled next to the intoxicating response she experienced as she felt his body against hers, the passion of his kisses deepening from moment to moment. Realizing how close she was coming to losing herself in his arms, she somehow forced herself to pull away.

He released her immediately. Unable to bring herself to look at his face, she turned away from him, and, with feelings of the deepest mortification for her behavior, covered her eyes with her hand.

"Shall we return to the house, then?" asked Darcy, his voice slightly unsteady.

She nodded, still avoiding looking at him. As they walked, she sought desperately for some comment to make light of the situation, but her thoughts were still too full of the sensation of his kisses.

"Miss Bennet, it seems I must make a habit of apologizing to you for my behavior. I would like to assure you that I do not usually engage in this sort of conduct, though I fear you would have every reason to disbelieve me under the circumstances; however, it is true, and I regret most sincerely having offended you."

"I thank you, sir, but I am not offended, except at my own behavior."

"Please, do not blame yourself in any way; I am completely at fault," Darcy responded, not without distress.

"That is most courteous of you to say, sir, but we both know that the conduct of neither of us, if strictly examined, was irreproachable."

"If so, I am still much more at fault than you." Tentatively, he asked, "Miss Bennet, I beg of you, if it is not too much to ask, to tell me what upsets you so much that you will not look at me?"

Taking a deep breath, Elizabeth crossed her arms in front of her and turned to regard him. In a pained voice, she asked, "What must you think of me?"

"You are concerned about what I think of you?" A relieved look lightened his face. "My dear Miss Bennet, I think of you as a virtuous young woman who I sincerely hope will be my future wife, and I count myself among the most fortunate of men that you apparently have enough feeling for me as to occasionally allow that feeling to overwhelm your sense of propriety where I am concerned. Please, you need feel no concern whatsoever on this subject."

"It is discomfiting, to say the least, that after never having allowed a gentleman even the slightest liberties in the past, I seem to have overnight begun to behave like my sister Lydia."

"Hardly, Miss Bennet, you have consistently applied restraint—"

Elizabeth interrupted, "Hardly consistently!"

He applied a look of mock disapproval to her before

continuing, "—whereas you would have every reason to think that I would stop at nothing to take advantage of you."

"I think not; the word 'no' seems to have been quite efficacious to date." She smiled rather tentatively at him, and was relieved to find that he returned her smile. With harmony somewhat restored, she added, "But I am, perhaps, not quite ready to face my family. I think I shall sit on this bench—in extremely full view of the house—for a few minutes yet, and I would be happy to have your company, sir."

He made a slight bow. They sat, and forcibly turned their conversation to safer topics, while Elizabeth made valiant but eventually futile attempts not to be completely distracted by the light touch of his hand against hers on the bench, a situation which to the casual observer would appear to be quite innocent, but which felt anything but that.

Chapter 5

As SOON AS THE gentlemen had taken their leave, Elizabeth, feeling quite unequal to any discussion regarding Darcy that might arise between her family members, took the opportunity to retire to her room to be alone with her thoughts. She was unsurprised, however, to hear a knock on the door heralding the arrival of Jane, full of concern for her well-being.

"Lizzy," said Jane, taking her hand, "what happened? Please, tell me all about it."

Elizabeth surprised herself and her sister by bursting into tears.

"Oh, Lizzy. I am so sorry. I hope he was not too cruel."

"No, he was not cruel. He said everything I could hope he would say. He was charming and solicitous…"

Jane, more than puzzled over her sister's distress, asked, "Did he renew his addresses?" In response to her sister's slight nod, she added, "And did you accept him?"

"I told him I needed time."

"Lizzy, why? Why not just accept him? You love him, I know you do!"

"Because, Jane, I do not have your touching faith in everyone's goodness, and I have learned to my chagrin that my judgments of people are not as accurate as I had always thought. I misjudged Darcy badly in the past in many ways. Now I am judging that he has changed greatly in regard to his pride, but I am choosing to believe this based on the evidence of five conversations. Five, Jane! Given my history of misjudgment, should I base my future happiness on what may be no more than a temporary aberration and a great deal of wishful thinking on my part? My heart wants to accept him, but my head tells me to be cautious."

"Bingley has known him and trusted him for years, Lizzy. That cannot count for nothing."

"I know, and Miss Darcy believes him to be the finest brother in the world, but I need evidence of my own."

"So you told him you needed time. Then what happened?"

Elizabeth, with a teary smile, said, "Then we progressed from behaving badly to behaving disgracefully, and then we had a fight over who was most at fault for it. Jane, you must *never* leave us alone together—we cannot be trusted."

"Dearest Lizzy, of course, if that is what you wish. But did you part well?"

"Yes, except for the stress of knowing that we both could

think of very little apart from how much we wished for the privacy to disgrace ourselves yet again! Oh, Jane, how do you and Bingley survive this longing and look so happy all the time? This is agony!"

Jane smiled gently. "The agony was all in the waiting and wondering for me. Perhaps, once you and Darcy have settled this between yourselves, it will be easier."

"And have you nothing to say of my behavior?"

"I am… surprised, but I do recognize that Darcy is a man who is violently in love, and I would imagine that he could be quite persuasive."

"Jane, you are too good for the rest of us!"

The comfort that Jane was able to offer allowed Elizabeth to face the rest of the day with tolerable composure, though her thoughts were continually at Netherfield, and sleep did not come easily that night.

Elizabeth awoke the next morning to the same thoughts and meditations which had at length closed her eyes. It was impossible to think of anything else but Darcy, and, after some period of being totally indisposed to employment, decided to start embroidering a new handkerchief with a pattern of intertwining forget-me-nots and sweet williams.

It was a relief when at last the gentlemen arrived. Bingley proposed their all walking out; it was agreed to, but Mary could not spare the time, and Kitty owned she was not much for walking. This plan being of eminent satisfaction to the four remaining walkers, they set out immediately.

Bingley and Jane soon tactfully lagged behind somewhat, allowing Elizabeth and Darcy to entertain each other. Elizabeth, with a sly glance at Darcy, informed him Jane was prepared to provide chaperonage for them, which engaged more laughter from him than she anticipated.

"You did not hear Bingley's original plan for the day," he said with great amusement. "He suggested—being tolerably well acquainted with how things stand for me—that we invite you and Jane to dine at Netherfield today, with the intent you and I could chaperone them, but in fact allow some small degree of privacy."

"Pray, how did you respond to this proposition, sir?"

"It is perhaps wisest for that to remain between Bingley and me," he replied, then, in response to a stern look from his companion, added, "But if you must know, I told him that I thought his plan to be ill-advised, in that it might lead to me reaching the altar before he did."

"Mr. Darcy!"

"So it is my expectation that Bingley will be keeping a close eye on us as well. I do seem to need all the help I can get in that regard," he said, continuing the banter. "But I hope your information did not give your sister an overly poor impression of me."

"Jane is constitutionally unable to think ill of anyone, and since you, sir, have already demonstrated your fine sensibilities in your choice of both Bingley and myself as favored companions, your place in her esteem is, I believe, quite secure."

"Well, if that is the case, perhaps I can afford to take a few risks." He turned and called back to his friend, "Bingley—the view behind us is most pleasant. You must show it to Miss Bennet."

As Elizabeth turned as well to see what he was pointing out, Darcy took advantage of the distraction of the other couple to steal a light but lingering kiss. "I never said Bingley would be a particularly *good* chaperone," he said with some satisfaction. "He has too much sympathy with my position."

"I hope you are aware that Jane does not," she replied, and, noting the continued inattention from their companions, very daringly reached up and brushed her lips against his.

His eyes darkened in response. "You are fortunate, Miss Bennet, in that I am sure our fine chaperones would intervene if I were to make the response I would wish to that."

Elizabeth laughed, and allowed her hand to slip lightly into his as they walked on. A few moments later, Jane called in a disapproving voice, "Elizabeth!"

Reluctantly, Darcy released her hand, saying, "I see you were correct, and she indeed has no sympathy whatsoever!"

"None, indeed," she replied. "Jane is far too good for the rest of us."

"I have been thinking," he said a few minutes later, "that when I return for Bingley's wedding, it is likely to be far more difficult to conceal my interest in you from your family, especially with my sister present."

"Not to mention the apparent likelihood of being caught in some compromising situation or other," she said demurely. "I did mention to Miss Darcy in my last letter that my parents think of you as only an indifferent acquaintance of mine, and that it would be best at present not to challenge that idea."

"Be that as it may, I would like to ask in all seriousness if you would object if, after my arrival for the wedding, I were to speak to your father regarding my intentions, with the understanding that I do not as yet have your consent."

Elizabeth was silent for a few moments as many feelings coursed through her. "I do not object, sir," she responded quietly.

"Do you approve?" There was a thread of tension in his voice.

She looked up to meet his intent gaze. "Yes, I approve. Perhaps you might tell him that we have… an understanding."

"Elizabeth," he breathed, his eyes drifting to her lips. Her pulses pounded in a now familiar sensation, and she found herself longing for the relief that only his touch could bring.

With a muttered curse, he glanced behind them, then drew her over into a copse of trees by the side of the path. "I make no apologies," he said in a low voice as he pulled her into his arms.

Secure in the knowledge that they would be shortly interrupted, Elizabeth allowed herself to slip her arms around his neck and abandon herself to the pleasure of his kisses. Tangling her fingers in his hair, she gasped as he drew a line of kisses along her cheek and down her neck before reclaiming her mouth once more with an urgency that stirred her beyond her imaginings.

"Elizabeth!" Jane cried. Reluctantly, they separated, and Elizabeth's guilty look and Darcy's unrepentant one met Jane's stern glare and Bingley's frankly delighted gaze. "I think it would be best if we all walked together."

As they meekly followed her sister, Darcy whispered in her ear, "If that was an example of what I have to look forward to with you, sweetest Elizabeth, I shall be a very happy man indeed." Elizabeth blushed furiously.

Darcy had promised to stop by Longbourn briefly to take his leave before his departure for Pemberley the following day, which provided a ray of hope for Elizabeth, who was already anticipating missing him. When he arrived, though, it became immediately clear there would be no opportunity for private conversation, as her mother insisted on commanding her attention for wedding plans. They were able to exchange a few heartfelt glances across the room, but no more. She still reserved hope for the moment of his departure, and was not the only one thinking of this; Bingley, when the moment came, announced himself to be too critical to the current discussion to break off, and perhaps Miss Elizabeth could see his guest to his carriage on his behalf.

Taking care to look none too anxious to perform this

task, she walked out into the hallway, followed by Darcy, who managed to find the briefest moment between their departure from the drawing room and the opening of the front door to press something into Elizabeth's hand. Then they were outside, in the presence of Darcy's footman and coachman, who stood with their eyes carefully averted as their master took his time kissing Miss Bennet's hand and thanking her for her most gracious hospitality while looking deeply into her eyes. She, in turn, assured him gravely of her hopes she would enjoy his company again soon. With one long parting look, he entered the carriage and was off. Elizabeth watched until it vanished from sight, trying to ignore the pricking of tears in her eyes, then, with a sigh, returned to the house. She paused inside just long enough to ascertain that what Darcy had given her was a paper, folded small, and she tucked it into her pocket for later perusal before returning to the drawing room.

After a certain amount of time spent entertaining Mr. Bingley and her family with a decidedly cheerful countenance, Elizabeth deemed it acceptable to retire to the safety of her room, where she at last was able to inspect the paper Darcy had given her.

Sonnet XCVII

How like a winter hath my absence been
From thee, the pleasure of the fleeting year!
What freezings have I felt, what dark days seen!

What old December's bareness every where!
And yet this time removed was summer's time,
The teeming autumn, but with rich increase,
Bearing the wanton burthen of the prime,
Like widow'd wombs after their lords' decease:
Yet this abundant issue seem'd to me
But hope of orphans and unfather'd fruit;
For summer and his pleasures wait on thee,
And, thou away, the very birds are mute;
Or, if they sing, 'tis with so dull a cheer
That leaves look pale, dreading the winter's near.

—W. Shakespeare

So shall I be until we meet again, my dearest Elizabeth, for you shall be my constant companion in thought, until I can be once more in your most beloved presence. Till then, I remain, as always, yours in every way, FD

Elizabeth, with deep feeling, pressed this missive to her breast, and it was some time before she could find the resolve to fold it up and secret it away in a drawer.

Had Elizabeth been aware of the exact time planned for Darcy's return to Hertfordshire, she would certainly have been counting the days, but as it was, she only knew that the next few weeks would be much longer than she would wish. She attempted, to the extent possible, to distract her mind with activity. When she found herself wakeful at night, she used the time to continue embroidering the handkerchief she intended for Darcy. During the day she spent a good deal of time in Jane's company, where she did not feel it necessary to pretend to a false cheerfulness.

She continued to be distressed by evidence of her family's dislike for Darcy. Her mother, while planning a dinner for Bingley, mentioned that at least it would be a more pleasant occasion since that proud, disagreeable Darcy would not be there, and Elizabeth was further troubled to find her father in rare agreement with her mother.

Jane glanced at Elizabeth, and said, "I quite like Mr. Darcy. He can be very charming, and as a close friend of my dear Bingley's, I am sure that I have nothing but good to say of him."

"Of course, you *must* like him, Jane, since he is Bingley's friend," responded Mr. Bennet, "but pray give the rest of us leave to dislike the man."

"Have you forgotten how he slighted Lizzy, and all his insufferable pride?" cried Mrs. Bennet. "Why Lizzy saw fit to invite his sister to visit is quite beyond my comprehension."

Elizabeth, who was beginning to wonder the same thing for a very different reason, ventured, "I have no quarrel with Mr. Darcy, and Miss Darcy is a very sweet girl. Do not forget that if she takes a liking to Mary and Kitty, she may well be able to put them in the way of some very wealthy men."

Mrs. Bennet, who had not thought of this most attractive prospect, cried, "Of course, what an excellent thought! Lizzy, do not forget she may be able to assist you in that regard, as well. You are not getting any younger, you know!"

Her daughter struggled hard not to smile as she said, "Perhaps, if I am truly fortunate, Miss Darcy might even have someone in mind for me already."

Although reassured Georgiana would receive a pleasant, if possibly overcivil, reception from her family, Elizabeth was nonetheless troubled by her parents' reaction to Darcy. She suspected the prospect of a son-in-law with all his wealth and grandeur would be enough to overcome her mother's abhorrence of the man, but she feared her father would be distressed by her choice. This unpleasant reflection eventually led her to solicit Jane, who was soon to go to London to make the final arrangements for her trousseau, to speak with the Gardiners requesting their support in improving Darcy's reputation with her parents.

Jane's departure, however, left Elizabeth without a confidante, an unhappy position she hoped would be relieved by the upcoming arrival of Miss Darcy, who would no doubt be more than happy to discourse with her on the subject of her brother. In the meantime, she made every effort to absent herself from her family when possible by means of long walks and errands in Meryton.

One day, after a return from such an expedition, she arrived home to the news that her mother had yet again confined herself to her rooms with a fit of nerves, and all Elizabeth's requests for information regarding the source of the crisis resulted in either giggles from Kitty or judgmental looks from Mary. Finally, with some exasperation, she went to the library to apply to her father regarding the matter.

"Ah, Lizzy, you are precisely the person I need to see. Please sit down," he greeted her.

"I was hoping, sir, you could explain to me what has led to my mother's distress in this latest instance."

"An interesting question, since you seem to be very much at the center of this," he said, and in response to Elizabeth's raised eyebrow, continued, "Apparently Hill, while cleaning your room today, made a certain discovery, which, then being represented to your mother, led to further search and further discovery. This in turn led to your mother's attack of nerves, and the job falling to me to inquire about the presence of certain items in your room."

Elizabeth's mind jumped immediately to Darcy's letters, and she felt a surge of anxiety that the long-delayed discussion was about to occur. "Which items do you have in mind, sir?"

Mr. Bennet produced Darcy's handkerchief and most recent note. Laying them down in front of her, he proceeded to drum his fingers lightly on his desk while watching her closely.

She found herself wishing desperately Darcy were beside her, or at Netherfield, and if not Darcy, at least Jane. She hated to see her father disappointed in her, his favorite child, but even for him, she was not prepared to forswear Darcy.

"Now, what am I to make of these?" he asked finally.

Elizabeth reverted to the use of her wit. "I have an admirer with excellent taste in poetry and a preference for fine linen."

Her father's lips twitched. "Perhaps, Lizzy, you would care to enlighten me somewhat further regarding this mysterious gentleman with the initials of FD."

Recalling with a start that Darcy signed the letter only with his initials, she debated with herself whether her father was in fact perfectly aware of his identity, or was truly in ignorance. Perhaps he considered Darcy such an unlikely candidate for her affections as not to be on a list of possibilities. If it were at all possible, she would prefer to postpone the confrontation regarding Darcy until she could face it with his support, and the possibilities for delay appealed to her mischievous side. "He is a young man from whom you will be hearing in good time, whose intentions are honorable, and whose resources will be sufficient to support me."

"And his name is…?"

"His name will certainly be a surprise to you when he approaches you."

Mr. Bennet, evidently amused by her evasions, said, "Lizzy, I have informed your mother that in light of your good sense, I can only assume that your anonymous friend is someone you met on your travels, perhaps in Kent. While I would have preferred to be approached by the gentleman in question before he began sending you compromising letters, I could perhaps overlook it if the circumstances warrant. I will warn you, however, that if by some unlikely chance your FD should prove to be a person of our acquaintance with those initials, you may safely assume that I will not look favorably on the match, given he is someone I can neither like nor respect. I find it hard to believe, however, that your judgment could fail you to such an extent."

She had not expected this level of disapproval. In increasing distress, Elizabeth confined herself to saying as calmly as possible, "It is my firm belief my choice is an impeccable one, and I will hope to eventually have your agreement on that. Apart from that, I will only say that I am resolved to act in that manner, which will, in my own opinion, constitute my happiness."

"Well, Lizzy, in that case, all I can say is I hope my faith in your good sense is not misplaced. I remind you that your mother may be less forgiving in the matter of your refusal to name names than I am."

"Of that I have no doubt," she said dryly as she took her leave of him, attempting to conceal her feelings of disappointment and resentment.

Irritably snatching up her bonnet, she strode outside, ignoring the calls of her sisters. She set off at a fast pace, not knowing in which direction she went, and at length found herself in the back corner of the gardens where she had so lately been with Darcy. Surrounded by her memories of his gentleness and passion, she attempted to face the painful reality of her father's words. To her surprise, she found her father's refusal to approve the match was exactly calculated to make her clearly understand her own wishes for the first time, and she admitted to herself at last that she would indeed offer Darcy a positive response to his proposals on his return, with or without the blessing of her family.

She could not, however, give up the matter of her father as hopeless. The Gardiners would be at Longbourn for the wedding, and she would beg them to intercede with Mr. Bennet on her behalf. Perhaps he would listen to their greater knowledge of Darcy, and with their support and Jane's, perhaps it might come to a satisfactory resolution after all.

"Lizzy!" Kitty ran up to her, bonnet askew and wind-blown. "There you are! You sly thing, why didn't you tell me? I would have helped you, just like I helped Lydia!"

Elizabeth, with a sigh, crossed her arms and looked heavenward in dismay.

"But who would have thought it? We all thought you so proper, and all the while you were meeting secretly with Denny!"

"With Denny?" Elizabeth asked in confusion.

"Did Father tell you that I was the one who figured it out? I knew his first name was Frederick, and I knew that he admired you, and then Father said, 'So that was the source of all her information about Wickham!' You should have seen his face!"

"Kitty," Elizabeth said with incredulity, "do you mean to say he thinks I have been having a liaison with Mr. Denny? Wickham's friend Denny?"

Kitty nodded excitedly.

"The one who helped cover up Lydia's elopement?" Elizabeth's disbelief went beyond words.

"Of course, but you were so sly! I never guessed, in all the times I saw you together, that you were partial to him. Oh, wait till Lydia hears!"

"If you will excuse me," Elizabeth said abruptly, and started back to the house in a fury. To think her father could even consider for a moment that she was accepting advances from Denny! Well, she would set him to rights, and have words to say about his faith in her judgment as well! At least she need not worry about how he would react to the truth; compared to the amoral and impoverished Denny, Darcy would seem positively heaven-sent.

The thought brought her to a sudden stop. Recalling all her parents' harsh words and ingrained prejudices about Darcy, the idea came to her that it might not be such a poor idea to let them continue to worry about the prospect of Denny as a son-in-law for a few days. By that point, her father might well be ready to welcome Darcy with open arms. A mischievous smile began to cross her face.

Chapter 6

IT WAS SOMETHING OF a revelation to Elizabeth to discover the extent to which she could enjoy deceiving her family. During the next two days, she sat through several harangues from Mrs. Bennet on the state of her nerves, moralistic lectures from Mary on the evils of loss of reputation, Kitty's constant pleas for details, and Mr. Bennet's concerned looks, to all of which she replied with a refusal to provide any further information and a smiling assurance that they had no cause for concern. When Mrs. Bennet began to threaten she would write to Mr. Gardiner and ask him to settle matters with Denny as he had with Wickham, Elizabeth could not restrain her laughter as she told her mother she was certain Mr. Gardiner would see no cause for concern in her involvement with FD. The frequent use of the word "shameless" as applied to her was further cause for her amusement.

Nonetheless, she had good intentions of confessing the truth once Miss Darcy arrived, feeling it would be quite unfair to her to expect her participation in the charade. While they were awaiting their guest, however, Mrs. Bennet announced that there would be absolutely no mention of Lizzy's shamelessness in front of Miss Darcy, thus relieving Elizabeth of the necessity of immediate confession—and the attendant scene Miss Darcy would witness—before her guest even had the opportunity to settle in.

Miss Darcy's arrival went smoothly; she was clearly pleased to see Elizabeth, and Mrs. Bennet's degree of overcivility did not seem to trouble her in the least. She was amiable with Kitty and Mary, though Elizabeth, with a slightly more experienced eye, could see she was, in fact, anxious about the interchange, but attempting to battle her shyness. Mary, who had heard so much about Miss Darcy's vaunted skill at the pianoforte that she was determined not to be outdone in civility as she was likely to be in music, insisted on taking Georgiana on the full tour of Longbourn and its grounds. Kitty, who was closest to her age, was delighted to keep her company as her trunks were unpacked, for the pleasure of remarking over each dress and bonnet as it emerged. By dinnertime they were all referring to each other by their first names. Between one sister and the other, it was near evening before Elizabeth had a chance to spend some time alone with Miss Darcy.

After they reassured one another of their delight in seeing the other, it was apparent to Elizabeth that Georgiana was still somewhat in awe of her, and very anxious to please. She attempted to put those anxieties to rest with warm inquiries about her time at Pemberley, their common acquaintances, and of course, Darcy. This led naturally to a rather timid question regarding Mr. and Mrs. Bennet's ignorance of Darcy's admiration of Elizabeth.

Elizabeth laughed. "Given the timing of your visit, you will very likely have the pleasure of witnessing exactly why I have allowed this state of affairs to persist. My parents, I am sorry to say, harbor some strong prejudices against your brother, and, though I have attempted to moderate their views, my success has been quite limited."

"When I said something to your sisters about what a good brother he is, they looked quite disbelieving! I did not know what to say."

"I am hardly surprised," Elizabeth said with a smile.

"But what reason could they possibly have to dislike him?"

"It is in fact quite an ironic story, in hindsight. It all began when he made a slighting comment about me at a public assembly, and refused to dance with me since I did not meet his standards."

"Oh," cried Georgiana. "So that is why he said that you…" she trailed off in embarrassment.

"Pray, now you have aroused my curiosity, what *did* he say?"

Georgiana blushed. "I shouldn't have said anything… it was a long time ago. He said that he had given you every reason to dislike him, and I couldn't understand what he could be talking about. I couldn't ask him about it, because that was when he was barely talking to anyone at all, and I knew I was lucky he had said as much as he did, but I always wondered what he meant."

"When was this?"

"Oh, after he returned from visiting Aunt Catherine last spring." The words began tumbling out of her, as if she had been barely holding them back for months. "It was so awful, Elizabeth! He was so quiet all the time, and if anyone asked him why, he would just stalk off, and he wouldn't even see his friends most of the time. If I tried to be sympathetic, he would tell me to save my pity for someone who deserved it, and then he'd try to put a good face on it, and that was even worse. And then, after a while, he seemed to just give up, and he didn't even get angry anymore; it was just as if he didn't care about anything anymore."

The pain Elizabeth felt on hearing this was as great as could be imagined. "I had no idea," she said with tears in her eyes. "I knew he must be angry and disappointed, but I assumed he would move on quickly—after all, there seemed to be no shortage of women who would be overjoyed to receive his addresses."

"Move on? How could you think that?" Georgiana asked. "Fitzwilliam *never* lets go of anyone, and he never stops caring."

"I am not certain I understand your meaning," Elizabeth responded cautiously.

"Haven't you noticed? He almost never lets himself care about anyone, but once he does, he is more loyal than anyone in the world. You have seen him with Bingley—since Bingley is his dear friend, he is willing to tolerate those horrible sisters of his—I know, I shouldn't say such things, but it's true—when any other man would have nothing to do with them. He puts up with Aunt Catherine, when I cannot even stand to be in the same room as her. He forgives everything in those he cares about—I should know—and never blames. If he had never seen you again, he would still have been hurt ten years from now, just like with…" Georgiana stopped short, her face frozen.

"Just like what?" Elizabeth asked gently, astonished by the insights she was receiving.

"Just like with George Wickham," Georgiana whispered, and burst into tears.

Elizabeth, feeling the greatest sympathy, moved rapidly to embrace the sobbing girl, murmuring words of comfort.

It took Georgiana several minutes to regain her composure. "I'm so sorry," she said. "I feel so awful when I think of how I hurt Fitzwilliam. I didn't know at the time, of course, but that makes no difference."

"My dear, please remember you are far from the only one taken in by Mr. Wickham. I myself believed his stories, and was charmed by him. All my family, indeed all of Meryton, delighted in him. You could not be expected to do more."

"But it wasn't so much what I did as what he did to my brother. How could anyone be so cruel?"

"What did he do to your brother?" asked Elizabeth with apprehension.

"I did not know the whole story then, because I had been too young when it happened, but afterward I started asking questions of people who knew him. Mrs. Reynolds told me most of this." She faltered for a moment. "He and Fitzwilliam were the best of friends when they were boys. As they became older, George apparently became resentful of the differences in their expectations, and began doing and saying terrible things to Fitzwilliam, but he was loyal and would never believe George did it on purpose. He caused trouble, knowing that Fitzwilliam would always try to cover up any problems he caused, even if it meant he himself was punished. The harder my brother would try to protect him and keep his friendship, the worse things George would do. This went on for years and years, until finally something must have been too much, I don't know what, but at some point even Fitzwilliam seemed to give up on him and started to avoid him, but even then he must have hoped that things might change in the future. The financial settlement he gave him was more than generous, I know. But then, the next time George approached him for help, Fitzwilliam refused, which had never happened before. And shortly thereafter, George tried to hurt him in the worst way he could, and he used me to do it. You would only need to have seen his face when he looked at George to see how pained he was that his old friend would do such a thing to him. But I shouldn't be telling you all this!"

"I'm very glad you did," Elizabeth said thoughtfully. "It helps me understand certain matters that have puzzled me in the past. Though I can only imagine how painful it was to watch Wickham deliberately hurt your brother, I must be clear with my opinion that *you* actually had little to do with it. If, as you say, his goal was to hurt your brother, he would simply have found another means of doing so had you been unavailable. I must say Wickham seems to show quite remarkable creativity in that regard."

"Someday I may even come to believe that myself, but you must have patience with me."

"Healing always does take patience, Georgiana, and healing from betrayal even more so."

"Elizabeth, I wish you really were my sister! Please, accept Fitzwilliam soon—he needs you so much!"

"I think that you need not worry; he and I are, I believe, quite close to reaching an agreement."

"But if your parents still dislike him so, what will they do when they find out?"

Elizabeth smiled. "Actually, I am currently engaged in a stratagem I believe will improve their outlook considerably," she told her in a conspiratorial tone. "The truth is I am currently in deep disgrace with my family, owing to the fact they have determined that I am engaged in a liaison with a militia officer of rather uncertain morals."

Georgiana's eyes grew wide, clearly unsure if she was serious or in jest, but Elizabeth relieved her mind immediately.

"They based this conclusion on finding in my possession a rather compromising letter signed with his initials, which happen to be FD. I have refused to comment on the matter, which is taken as a sign of guilt, but I believe that by the time they discover that FD is your brother, they will be so relieved he is not Mr. Frederick Denny all the ill will of the past will be forgotten!"

Georgiana clapped her hand over her mouth in surprise, then burst into delighted giggles. "No, you are teasing me. I cannot believe it!"

"I am afraid it is quite true—I'm sure Kitty or Mary would be happy to fill you in on the details of my supposed affair. But you should feel no need to participate in the fiction; sooner or later I will have to tell them the truth."

"I won't say a word!" Georgiana's eyes gleamed. "I might even have a bit more compromising material, if you need it." She drew out a well-sealed envelope and handed it to Elizabeth. "I was told very strictly only to give this to you when I was sure we were alone."

With a laugh, Elizabeth assured her that Darcy would soon be accusing her of corrupting his little sister if she started participating in such conspiracies, a description which made Georgiana giggle even more.

❧

Elizabeth made no effort to find privacy to read her letter, and even on retiring for the night, found herself merely taking it out and looking at it without opening it. She ran her fingers lightly over the Darcy seal, conscious of feeling she did not deserve to receive any recognition from him at all.

How little she really knew him! And how great, apparently, was his devotion to her. Recalling Georgiana's description of his despair after her refusal, tears began to fall down her cheeks. She had wondered about his disappointment, but it never occurred to her she might have caused him lasting distress. How she wished she had been more temperate in her words that day at Hunsford, that she had given him a chance to explain instead of pouring out her anger at him! A vivid memory came to her of Darcy's face when she accused him on Wickham's behalf—what worse could she have done? She did not deserve him, she thought to herself, but she would do everything in her power to make certain she never hurt him again. Gently, she broke the seal and opened the letter.

My dearest Elizabeth,

I feel I have so much to tell you, yet when I try to set it down, I find that I am, as the poet says, "as an imperfect actor on the stage who with his fear is put beside his part," and so am I "oe'rcharged with burden of mine own love's might," and have not the words to express my thoughts. You are in my mind at every moment, and whenever anything of import happens, I find myself wondering what you would say, what you would think, if you were beside me. As I walk, I notice the sights around me as if for the first time, and hope that they will please you. I know it to be selfish of me, but I feel as if you somehow belong at Pemberley—as if Pemberley itself will not be complete until you are here, yet I know myself to be the one who feels incomplete without you. I miss the sound of your voice, the look in your eyes, your laugh—and I am certain you know which memories haunt my nights.—It causes me to wonder what has happened to the Darcy of the past who would never have violated proprieties so much as to write such a line, much less have given cause for the same, and all I can know is that he vanished when you first smiled on me.—I envy Georgiana, that she will have the privilege of being in your presence, while I must remain here without you. Until we meet again, know that all my love and devotion are yours.

Fitzwilliam Darcy

She shed a few more tears over her letter, thinking how fortunate she was to have not only gained his love in the first place, but also to be given another, much undeserved chance. She took a deep, somewhat ragged breath, and knew what it was she needed to do.

Picking up a lamp, she walked downstairs to the library where she knew Mr. Bennet would, by habit, be reading late into the night. She knocked lightly on the door, and entered in response to his call.

He looked at her inquisitively over his glasses, not putting aside his book. "Yes, Lizzy?"

Taking a deep breath, she said, "Fitzwilliam Darcy."

"What about him?"

She glanced heavenward for a moment, asking for patience. "FD. Fitzwilliam Darcy."

Mr. Bennet carefully laid down his book and removed his glasses. "Are you attempting to suggest *Mr. Darcy* sent you that... love note?" he asked with a certain degree of incredulity.

Elizabeth lifted her chin. "That is indeed the case."

"Lizzy," he said, looking grave, "are you out of your senses, to be accepting the attentions of that man? Have not you always hated him?"

How earnestly did she then wish that her former opinions had been more reasonable, her expressions more moderate! "There was a time when I would have said so, but for some time I have felt... quite differently."

"Or in other words, you are determined to have him. He is rich, to be sure, and you may have more fine clothes and fine carriages than Jane. But will they make you happy?"

"I would marry him if he hadn't a penny, and, while I would prefer to marry him with your blessing, the lack of it will not stop me."

He observed her silently for a few moments. "Well, Lizzy, I confess you have truly surprised me. I cannot think of any man of our acquaintance who I would consider a less likely candidate to win your affections."

"Nonetheless, that is the situation."

"I see." He paused. "May I ask who else may be aware of this?"

"The Gardiners have known for some time, and more recently, Jane and Bingley. Miss Darcy as well, of course."

"You told the Gardiners, and they said nothing of it to me?" he said with deceptive mildness.

"It was more a matter of their discovering it than being told," she said, smiling slightly at the memory. "And, if I am not mistaken, Mr. Gardiner tried to say something of it to you, but you disbelieved him."

"So I did," he said thoughtfully. "Well, Lizzy, what would you have me do?"

She sighed in relief at this attempt to meet her halfway. "I would ask that you try to get to know him, with an open mind, remembering much of your unfortunate impression of him is based on Wickham's lies."

"That seems a fair enough request. What do you plan to tell your mother?"

"Nothing," Elizabeth responded with heartfelt sentiment. "Not until I have to."

Mr. Bennet gave an ironic smile. "Well, I shall keep this matter between the two of us until you tell me otherwise. Lizzy, you have given me a great deal to think about, and perhaps we can discuss this further when I have had the opportunity to do so."

"I would like that," she said, turning to leave.

"And Lizzy? I'm glad that you told me."

Elizabeth, with a strong sense of relief, said, "So am I."

Chapter 7

ELIZABETH, HER ANXIETY MUCH reduced following her discussion with Mr. Bennet, found herself over the next few
days doing nothing so much as waiting for Darcy's return.
She walked out with Georgiana on occasion, showing her
the sights of Meryton and its vicinity, helped with wedding
preparations, calmed her excitable mother, and otherwise
seemed full of activity, but her thoughts had only one goal.

She spent less time with her guest than she would have
expected, since Georgiana quickly formed an alliance with
Mary and Kitty. Elizabeth was fascinated to observe the interactions between the three very diverse young women. Kitty
was much taken with Georgiana's graceful ways, and set to
imitating them as assiduously as she ever had Lydia's wildness,
while Georgiana seemed drawn into some of Kitty's liveliness.
Mary, finding Georgiana respectful of her accomplishments,
and, much to her surprise, not above asking for her assistance

and advice with her music, seemed to feel more confident of herself; and while the younger girl was more than happy to spend hours reading with Mary, she pushed hard for reading poetry and novels over sermons. Elizabeth doubted the efficacy of this until she came across Mary reading a romantic novel one day, which Mary defensively informed her was one that Georgiana had praised. Mary found it hard to ignore when Kitty and Georgiana went off into long discussions on fashions and hairstyles, and eventually was pressed into developing some small interest in the topic herself so as not to be left out, causing the other two to coax her into making some small, but flattering, changes in her hair and manner of dress.

Elizabeth, pleased to hear the constant conversations, laughing and romping between the three, on occasion found herself feeling more like an aunt than an elder sister. It seemed likely to her that Georgiana's previous shy and quiet behavior might have been related to being always surrounded by persons much older than herself, and to her constant awareness of her complicity in the Ramsgate affair.

She also suspected, based on a certain amount of giggling apparently directed toward her, that keeping secrecy became too difficult for Georgiana, and that her sisters had been let in on the news of Darcy's interest in her as well. Mr. Bennet had turned out to have very little to say on the subject of Darcy after their late-night talk, beyond once asking Elizabeth when she had come to change her opinion of him.

One day, some five days before Darcy was expected—as

Elizabeth kept track of time—Mary, Kitty, and Georgiana walked out to Meryton. Mrs. Bennet visited Mrs. Philips, leaving Elizabeth with time enough to enjoy the unseasonable warmth of the day by collecting fall fruits from the garden for a centerpiece. She found herself particularly taking pleasure in the quiet of the gardens, knowing Jane and the Gardiner family would be arriving from London on the following day, and she could expect little more peace until after the wedding. Allowing herself to luxuriate in the feeling of the sun on her shoulders and the gentle breeze, she was sublimely unaware of the presence of an interested observer.

Darcy found himself captivated by the image of Elizabeth, the sunlight gilding her hair, as she passed gracefully from the small orchard into the vineyard. He watched with longing the dance of her precise, calm movements as she clipped clusters of grapes, allowing them to drop gently without bruising into her waiting hand, then transferring them to the basket. Her exposed neck as she bent over seemed to beg for his kisses, and he controlled himself only by gripping the trellis beside him with sufficient force to cause his hand to ache.

Finally he brought himself to speak her name. He saw her become still at the unexpected sound of his voice, then she turned to face him, her eyes alight, wreaking havoc with his every intention of composure.

Elizabeth, taken unawares, felt a not unpleasant sense of agitation. "Mr. Darcy," she said. "This is a most pleasant surprise."

"Not 'Mr. Darcy,' Elizabeth. Not to you."

Elizabeth felt breathless. "Fitzwilliam," she said softly, feeling both shy and extraordinarily alive.

He willed his hands to stay still. Mesmerized by the sparkle in her fine eyes, he could find no words to express the eagerness he felt just being near her. She took his breath away.

As the silence drew on, her mouth twitched in amusement. "Perhaps we should begin this conversation anew, sir. I could say, 'Why, I did not expect you for some days yet,' to which you could reply with an acknowledgement of your change in plans; I could inquire about your journey, and you might ask about the well-being of your sister."

Amused, he decided that two could play at this game. "Then, perhaps, you could report to me about the success of her visit, and I could tell you just how long I have been waiting and hoping to have you greet me with just that look in your eyes, how even last year when you stayed at Netherfield, I would watch when your eyes would light up with pleasure, and wish most fervently such a look could be for me."

"Even then? I thought you watched me only with intent to find fault."

"To find fault? I cannot imagine why; I would have thought it obvious I watched you because it gave me the greatest of pleasure."

Elizabeth laughed. "My aunt Gardiner says you and I have a talent for misconstruing each other. I am glad to see we are both improving in our understanding."

"As long as I am not misconstruing my welcome, I am

quite content." How was he to keep from touching her when she looked so beguiling? It was hopeless. He reached out and caught her hand, but instead of providing relief, her touch merely increased his desire.

Elizabeth's mouth went dry. With an attempt at control, she said with a degree of desperation, "I believe you may feel quite secure in your welcome, but we do face a problem, sir, in that everyone aware of our need for chaperonage is presently in London."

He smiled meaningfully. "Yes, I am quite aware of that; as I called on the Gardiners yesterday when I was in town."

"Ah. I must assume you are very brave, then, to dare to approach me," she said lightly, her heart pounding so fiercely she felt sure he must be able to hear it.

"Hardly brave, my dearest. Remember that, having already lost my heart to you, I have nothing left to lose." He touched her cheek lightly with his fingertips, then moved them lightly along her hairline and down the sensitive skin of her neck. "After all, the worst I could face would be your father, who would demand that I marry you immediately, to which I would say…" he paused, his eyes fixed on his fingers as they continued to trace their way agonizingly slowly along the line of her exposed collarbone, "…would tomorrow be soon enough, because if not…" His lips found their way to a delicate caress of her neck. "…I am quite at leisure this afternoon."

Aroused to the point of distraction by his touch, she gave a small, inarticulate moan, and put her hands to his shoulders to steady herself. Stirred even further by this encouragement, Darcy continued his exploration of her arched neck and the crevices of her shoulders with his lips until, unable to withstand his need any longer, he sought her mouth with his own.

The delicate control Darcy had shown in touching her earlier dissolved in the increasing urgency of his kisses. She shivered as his hand stroked down her back, and, arching her body against his, surrendered to the demands of his mouth. Her hands crept up around his neck, then buried themselves in his hair. He held her tightly, inflamed by the depth of her response. The passion her touch evoked in him went beyond his furthest imaginings.

As he turned the attention of his lips to her face, Elizabeth could not stop herself from whispering his name with the deepest of longing. Feeling completely undone by the passion he had awakened in her, she could only abandon herself to the pleasure his touch induced in her with no thought for the future.

With a groan, Darcy lifted his lips and pulled her head against his shoulder. Burying his face in her hair, he whispered, "You are everything I have ever dreamed of."

Elizabeth, trembling, found herself leaning against him for support as she sought, with no great success, to collect herself.

Within the security of Darcy's arms, Elizabeth struggled to recover from the uncontrollable feelings his kisses had aroused in her. She was all too aware it was only his self-restraint that had prevented the situation from going any further beyond the bounds of propriety than it already had. With some discomfiture, she said, "Well, Mr. Darcy, we seem to have obtained evidence which suggests that any inadequacies in your self-control have been greatly overrated."

"I endeavor to keep surprising you," he said, a slight unsteadiness in his voice betraying the battle he was fighting. "I hope that I did not… alarm you with my attentions."

"I am far more embarrassed than alarmed, and I certainly do not hold you responsible for that," she said. She had never allowed him just to hold her before, and she was astonished by the contentment she felt in his arms.

He kissed her hair. "My dearest Elizabeth, if you only knew how very gratifying and reassuring your behavior is to me, you might feel less embarrassed—you might even look upon it as a charitable effort on your part."

"An excellent idea!" Elizabeth laughed, looking up at him, but making no move to leave his arms. "Having failed at my studies of patience and self-control, I should begin work on a new virtue, and charity—at least by your definition of it!—seems to be something I manage to practice whether I intend to or not."

"You may practice on me to your heart's content, Miss Bennet, so long as you wait until my self-control is at least slightly more in evidence than it is at this moment."

She smiled. "I may play with fire, sir, but I try to steer clear of bonfires." Some of his earlier words came back to her.

"But I would hope you do not stand in any particular need of charitable reassurance from me."

He was silent for a moment, but she could feel his tension. "Elizabeth, please recall that only a few months ago you considered me the last man of your acquaintance you could be prevailed upon to marry. While evidence indicates your opinion of me has improved—I would hope that by now I would rate above, say, Mr. Collins as a marital partner—reassurance is always welcome, and often needed."

"Must you remember so well everything I said that awful day?" Elizabeth asked with chagrin.

He allowed his hands to caress her for a moment. "Please do not distress yourself over the past, my dearest; some of your words have proved quite memorable, but I seem to recall saying more than my share of such words!"

"Then I must strive for even more memorable ones to suit the present situation."

He gave the slight smile which always tugged at her heart. "I am all ears, my sweetest Elizabeth."

She pulled away from him just far enough that she could look into his eyes. "Is this sufficiently memorable?" she said, her heart beating rapidly. "Mr. Darcy, I would be delighted and most honored to become your wife."

His first reaction was disbelief, for since his overconfidence in Kent, he had never allowed himself to fully believe he would ever earn her consent. This was followed immediately by a feeling of heartfelt delight such as he had never before felt. *She will be mine!* he thought. *She will make me complete again.* He swallowed hard as an image from his dreams came to him—Elizabeth, her eyes full of passion, in his bed and in his arms—merging with the sensation of the very real woman he held in his arms. He said unsteadily, "I believe the traditional response is to tell you that you have made me the happiest of men, but even those words cannot do justice to how very, very happy you have made me."

"Well, let us not defy tradition, although, were we to be strictly traditional, I should have waited to be asked before supplying my answer!"

Taking her face between his hands, he kissed her deeply and possessively, the kind of kiss that claims a bond rather than overwhelms with passion. "Elizabeth, my own, so long as you never leave me, I will say anything you wish, but I believe you are well aware of my hopes and wishes."

"There is nothing you need to say, Fitzwilliam," she said softly, allowing herself the pleasure of touching his cheek lightly.

His eyes ignited with a familiar look, and she could see the battle he was fighting with himself. "There is one more thing…" he began, then faltered as Elizabeth, smiling provocatively, slid her arms around his neck, "…which we can discuss later," he concluded in a somewhat strangled voice as he responded in the only possible way.

Had Elizabeth thought his passion would be in some way more controlled with his better understanding of her regard for him, she would have had to revise that opinion quite rapidly as his fiery kisses burned her lips with unrestrained ardor. She found that what had begun with an affectionate and intimate gesture on her part rapidly turned into a conflagration in which her passion rose to meet his. She felt lost in a flood of sensation as he explored her mouth, and, as he moved his attention to her face and her neck, she found herself arching her head back to allow further liberties.

Darcy, having unwisely allowed himself to imagine his nights with Elizabeth, found those thoughts had wrought havoc with his self-restraint. He felt all resolve melt as Elizabeth gave into the temptation to allow her fingers to roam through his hair and over the exposed skin of his neck. His lips fully occupied with investigating the hollows over her collarbone, he found his hands seeking to explore the gentle curves of her spine.

Elizabeth's involuntary gasp of pleasure brought her attention back to herself, and, with a Herculean effort of will, she sought to extricate herself from his embrace, and laid her fingers lightly over his lips. Meeting his eyes, dark with passion, almost destroyed her resolve, but she somehow managed to maintain her distance.

Darcy forced his breathing to slow. "I hope you are not planning to insist on a long engagement," he said.

"That would appear to be unwise," Elizabeth allowed, sounding a good deal calmer than she felt.

"Then perhaps we should take appropriate steps," he

said softly. He removed a small box from his pocket, and, taking her hand, opened it to show her a ring of sapphire and diamond. "I was carrying this when I called on you at the inn in Lambton," he said as he slid it slowly onto her finger. "My father gave this to my mother when he asked her to be his wife."

The sight of the ring on her hand brought her a new sense of the truth of their engagement, and she found herself thinking of all the changes it would bring to her life. Darcy's thoughts ran along a similar path; the physical reality of her acceptance of his ring made it true that she would be his, that he had at long last won her love. He lifted her hand to his lips, then held it gently to his cheek in a gesture of trust which touched Elizabeth deeply.

"Your mother must have been a very fortunate woman," said Elizabeth shakily.

"They were both fortunate," he responded softly. "My parents had an exemplary marriage, full of affection and respect. I have always told myself I would settle for nothing less."

Elizabeth's breath caught in her throat. "I hope I will live up to your faith in me."

With a slight smile, he said, "I have no doubts of your success. We do, however, have a few matters to resolve regarding our wedding, and I believe I have a somewhat overdue meeting with your father as well. Perhaps there is a place where we could sit while we talk?"

Elizabeth gave him an arch look. "Always assuming that

we could behave ourselves long enough to resolve anything?" With a smile, she led him to a shaded bench across the garden.

"I do not recall making any promises about behaving myself," Darcy said as they sat. Suiting his actions to his words, he took her hands in his and brushed his lips lightly across hers. "I believe I can manage to hold a conversation between kisses, and if it should prove distracting to you, so much the better for making plans to my liking."

"And may I ask what those plans would be?" asked Elizabeth.

A playful look entered his eyes. "I thought the idea of getting married this afternoon had a good deal of merit," he said with an innocent air.

Elizabeth laughed. "I fear that is hardly possible, sir. There is no time to obtain a license, and my mother would never forgive me if I married in an everyday dress. I am afraid you will need to wait at least a few days!" she teased in return.

"I cannot help with the matter of your dress, except to say I would find you beautiful in sackcloth. As to the other matter…" He withdrew a paper from his pocket and held it up teasingly between two fingers.

Elizabeth looked at him suspiciously as she took the document. Unfolding it, she was taken aback to find it to be a special license, issued in their names the previous day at Doctors' Commons. "You cannot be seriously suggesting…" she said with some disbelief.

"I believe I could force myself to wait as long as a week, given proper incentives."

"But that is when Jane and Bingley are to be wed!"

"We could have a double ceremony."

"How could we be ready in a week?"

"You are being far too argumentative," he replied with a mocking threat in his voice, and proceeded to run his finger seductively beneath her neck. "I see I shall have to distract you after all." He proceeded to trail a line of light kisses from her ear to the base of her neck. Elizabeth bit her lip in an attempt to deny him the satisfaction of seeing her response. "Now, about that double ceremony…"

"You cannot be serious!"

He traced her cheek with his finger. "More so than you think, my loveliest Elizabeth, but not without reason. To explain, however, I will need to ask you to keep a secret from the future Mrs. Bingley."

"As long as I do not consider it to be doing her a disservice, you may rely on me."

"I rely on you constantly, my sweetest. But to the subject at hand, last week I received one of Bingley's illegible letters telling me it was his intention to surprise your sister with a honeymoon on the continent—more specifically, spending the winter in Italy."

Elizabeth's eyes lit up. "Oh, Jane will love that! She has always wanted to travel."

"Knowing how close you and she are, I knew you would want her to attend our wedding. Since we will *not* be waiting six months to marry"—he gave her a pointed look to indicate the nonnegotiability of his statement—"this leaves the choice between a hurried wedding attended by Jane now, or a more leisurely one without her later. Hence my trip to London, where I consulted with Bingley regarding a possible delay to their departure plans, and my early arrival here, so as to be able to offer you the choice in the matter. The double ceremony was Bingley's suggestion. Alternatively, Bingley feels they could delay their departure up to a week after their wedding to give us more time.

"Next week?" Elizabeth said faintly. It had never occurred to her that Jane might not be at her wedding, and she felt grateful to Darcy for his consideration.

"You are repeating yourself, my dearest," Darcy said, allowing his lips to explore her hair with complete disregard for his own ability to concentrate.

"You were very confident of my acceptance, it seems," she said.

"It would be more accurate to say I was hopeful, and I confess to enough impatience that the idea of having to marry sooner rather than later has a certain appeal to me." He paused to steal a quick kiss. "I understand that you may have other priorities, however; it is more of a change for you than for me."

"I don't know..." Feeling somewhat overwhelmed by the change he was proposing, she let her head rest against his shoulder.

Darcy's attention seemed distracted for a moment. "Have you told your mother about us yet?" he asked.

"No, she has no idea, though I have discussed it with my father."

"I fear that she may have just found out," he said.

Elizabeth turned quickly to see Mrs. Bennet retreating rapidly toward the house in the company of Mrs. Philips, who was clearly offering consolation to her distressed friend. Closing her eyes, she took a deep breath. "I had best go to her, then," she said with some trepidation, knowing the scene to follow had the potential to become quite unpleasant and undignified. "Perhaps you could return to speak with my father this evening."

"I think there is no time like the present, and I certainly do not wish to leave you to face the inquisition on your own."

Reluctantly, she said, "To tell the truth, this is likely to be embarrassing at best, and likely much worse, and I would prefer not to subject myself to the mortification of having you watch it."

He touched her cheek. "Elizabeth, I can tolerate your mother. Please have faith in me."

This being an approach Elizabeth would have been hard put to reject, she agreed to allow him to accompany her. He paused only to kiss her lightly. "Remember that I love you," he murmured in her ear.

She turned and looked steadily at him. "I depend upon it," she replied.

"As I depend on you, my sweetest, loveliest Elizabeth."

Chapter 8

"Oh, Mr. Bennet, you are wanted immediately; we are all in an uproar! You have no idea what has happened," cried Mrs. Bennet. "You must come and make Mr. Darcy marry Lizzy!

"Mr. Darcy! Madam, I doubt I could make Mr. Darcy give me the time of day, if he were not so inclined, so I would hesitate to believe that I could make him marry anyone, least of all Lizzy, for whom you have always told me he has had the greatest indifference!"

"Nonsense, how can you talk so! You take delight in vexing me! They are just now in the garden together, and, oh, Mr. Bennet, what shall we ever do?"

"You may tell him from me, madam, that he has my full permission to be in the garden whenever he chooses, and that should put an end to the matter!"

Unable to contain herself, Mrs. Bennet cried in vexation.

"You have no compassion for my poor nerves! And what shall become of poor Lizzy?"

The subjects of the conversation chose this moment to make their appearance, having overheard the previous remarks. Darcy, with his most correct social manner covering what to Elizabeth was obviously repressed laughter, bowed most correctly to his hostess. "Mrs. Bennet, a pleasure to see you again. And do I recollect that this is your sister? It has been far too long, madam." Without allowing time for anyone else to speak, he turned to Mr. Bennet. "Mr. Bennet, would it be possible for me to speak with you privately regarding a matter of some importance?"

Mr. Bennet looked him up and down. "Well, Mr. Darcy, I cannot imagine what you would have to say to me that would be of any import, but you are welcome to join me in the library, where it is certainly much quieter. I understand you have already taken a tour of the gardens."

Darcy cast Elizabeth a look of amused apprehension as he disappeared with her father. Taking a deep breath, she turned to face her mother.

"Lizzy!" Mrs. Bennet wailed. "How could you do this to us! Have you no regard for my nerves? You will disgrace us all!"

Lizzy pressed her lips together to hide a smile. "I am sorry to hear that. I certainly hope that any disgrace of mine will not dissuade Mr. Darcy, since we have only just become engaged. He is asking my father for my hand as we speak."

The effect of this communication was quite extraordinary,

for on hearing it, Mrs. Bennet found herself quite unable to utter a syllable. She managed to recover herself under the excited ministrations of Mrs. Philips, and expressed herself in such a tumult of joy as to make Elizabeth exceedingly grateful for Darcy's absence. She could not give her consent, or speak her approbation in terms warm enough to satisfy her feelings.

"Good gracious! Lord bless me! Only think! Mr. Darcy! Who would have thought it! And is it really true? Oh, my dear Lizzy! Pray apologize for my having disliked him so much before. I hope he will overlook it. Dear, dear Lizzy. A house in town! Everything that is charming! Three daughters married! Ten thousand a year! Oh, Lord! What will become of me, I shall go distracted."

❧

"Well, Mr. Darcy, what can I do for you today?" asked Mr. Bennet.

"Sir, I would like to ask for the honor of your daughter's hand in marriage," Darcy said formally.

"Ah, yes, Lizzy. A bit overdue in approaching me, aren't you?"

"Your daughter can be difficult to convince, sir."

"By you? Not that I would have noticed, Mr. Darcy. But no matter—the question is why are you asking my consent?"

Darcy paused, puzzled. He had thought his request perfectly clear. "I would like your consent to marry your daughter."

"Yes, yes, you want to marry Lizzy; that shows fine taste on your part, if a certain degree of disregard for your own peace of mind. But I fail to see where *I* come into this."

"Sir, I do not have the honor of following your meaning."

"Well, then, Lizzy has told me she plans to marry you with or without my consent, so it seems that there is no need to ask it, is there?"

"Your daughter says a good many things, Mr. Bennet, but she does not speak for me; *I* would like to have your consent."

"You would like that, would you? And will it stop you if I fail to give my consent?" Mr. Bennet asked affably.

Darcy steepled his fingers and was silent for a minute. "No, sir, it will not."

"Then it certainly seems to be a waste of your time and energy to be debating the issue with a difficult old man!"

Darcy was beginning to understand the source of Elizabeth's playful sense of humor. "Possibly, sir, but I consider it good practice for dealing with your daughter."

"Point taken, young man. So, why should I give you permission to marry Lizzy? I believe we can skip over the discussion of your material prospects, and I am willing to take your tender regard for her as a given." Mr. Bennet sat back, clearly relishing the discussion.

"Among other things, it would improve your family harmony; I speak from experience when I say that Miss Elizabeth can be quite stubborn when she sets her mind to it, and she seems to be quite set on marrying me."

Mr. Bennet waved this away. "I am quite accustomed to dealing with familial disharmony."

"Perhaps then you should speak to your wife. She seems to feel that I have compromised your daughter, and as such, I obviously should marry her."

"Oh, ho, so that is how the land lies, is it? Is there something you ought to be telling me about?"

Darcy leaned forward, and said with great deliberation, "Only this, sir, that I am prepared to sit here and argue this with you all day and all night if need be, until you give your consent simply to be rid of me."

The two stared at each other. Finally Mr. Bennet chuckled. "Very well, young man. I see you have enough mettle to handle my Lizzy. You have my consent."

"I thank you, sir, and I believe you will have no cause to regret your decision."

"Well, we shall see, I would imagine."

Darcy found himself not quite ready to quit the battlefield without having fired a shot of his own. "Sir, I do have one question."

"Yes, what is it?"

"I understand from my friend Bingley that he found asking your permission to marry Miss Bennet a simple and straightforward procedure. This seems rather different from my experience. Perhaps you might explain this to me."

"You are not reticent, sir! Very well, if you wish to know,

when Jane brings home a puppy dog, I pat its head. When Lizzy brings me a full-grown wolf, I handle it differently."

Darcy inclined his head. "I see we understand one other, sir."

"Yes, yes, and I am sure you would rather be spending your time with Lizzy than with me, so be off with you!"

"Sir." Darcy stood and gave him a very correct bow before leaving.

He found Elizabeth awaiting him anxiously in the drawing room. "Well?" she asked.

Darcy sank gratefully into a chair. "There are thousands of fathers in England who would be delighted to have me ask for their daughter's hand."

Elizabeth bit her lip. "He was difficult, then? Did he give his consent?"

"Yes, he was difficult, and yes, he consented, though only after I had threatened him with family discord, loss of reputation, and holding him hostage. Apart from that, it went quite well."

Elizabeth laughed. "You should probably feel complimented; he is truly only difficult when he has a positive view of a matter."

"Did you really tell him you would marry me with or without his consent?"

Elizabeth blushed. "Does that shock you, sir?"

He gave her a sidelong look. "Terribly. I believe I shall require a great number of kisses to recover from the experience."

"Fortunately, I believe that you know where to find them, sir," she said.

"Your perception astonishes me, Miss Bennet," he said, rising to move behind her chair. As she looked up at him, he bent to give her a series of slow, gentle kisses.

"Is that better, Mr. Darcy?" she asked archly as he released her mouth.

"Not yet." He proceeded to feather a series of kisses behind her ear, traveling slowly to the nape of her neck which had so enticed him when he first saw her in the vineyard earlier. She shivered as he moved his lips ever so slowly along the length of the back of her neck and the soft skin exposed by the neckline of her dress, and felt a need she could not understand growing within her. Darcy could clearly sense her growing tension, and when he finally allowed his mouth to approach hers again, they met with a deep hunger that could not be denied.

The sound of laughing voices raised in lively conversation began to intrude, and Darcy jumped back, straightening, just before the room was invaded by Georgiana, Kitty, and Mary. Georgiana stopped short when she saw her brother, then rushed to embrace him. "Fitzwilliam! I did not expect to see you so soon! What a lovely surprise!"

"You are looking very well. Your visit seems to have agreed with you, my dear," he replied.

"I have had the best time! You know Mary and Kitty, don't you? We have had such fun. Mary likes to practice a great deal as well, and we have been helping each other with our music, haven't we, Mary? We've prepared a new duet that I think you will like."

"I am very glad to hear it. Georgiana, would you care to greet your new sister?"

Georgiana's eyes grew wide. "Lizzy!" she squealed, throwing her arms around her. "At last! Oh, I'm so happy for you both! I'll be so glad to have you as a sister. It will feel like getting a whole family of sisters," she said, glancing at the others.

She continued to chatter on to Darcy about everything she had done during her visit, with assists from Mary and Kitty. Darcy gave Elizabeth an inquisitive but not displeased look as he took in his sister's altered behavior.

❦

As dusk was approaching, Darcy, whose good temper was starting to fray from the social demands of the Bennet family, took the opportunity to ask Elizabeth to walk out with him, which she gratefully accepted. They were mostly silent as they walked; after all the emotions of the day, Elizabeth felt more agitated and confused than happy, and Darcy found he had much to think about. At the top of a rise which would afford a view of the upcoming sunset Elizabeth led them to a small arbor with a rude bench carved from a fallen log. She settled herself and invited him to do the same.

"Georgiana seemed in a remarkable mood this afternoon," Darcy said thoughtfully.

"I had been under the impression she tended to be quiet and shy, but we have seen very little of that here, to say the least. Of course, I have not spent as much time with her as I expected, since she and my sisters have been so taken with each other—to the benefit of all three, I might add—but she has been quite talkative and playful since she settled in."

"That is indeed remarkable. Although she was quite animated as a child, after our father died she seemed to become more serious, and since the events of last summer, has been somewhat withdrawn as well. Perhaps she needed to escape from all the reminders of the past."

She considered this. "I think the company of girls her own age is helpful as well. Perhaps she tried too hard to be an adult before she is ready. She also spoke to me about Wickham at one point; I was impressed with her insights into the situation."

"I confess I am relieved to hear she talked to you about it; I have worried she keeps too much of her feelings to herself."

Elizabeth smiled. "She worries about you, as well. I think she may be feeling relieved she can turn over the task of worrying about you to me."

"Shall you worry about me, then?" he teased.

"I am certain the occasion will arise at some point."

He shifted closer to her and gathered her to him so her back rested against his chest. She leaned her head back against him, enjoying the comfort of his closeness.

"Have you thought any further about the question of our wedding?" he asked, playing with her fingers.

Elizabeth sighed. "A little; it is confusing, though. There is much to be said for next week, yet at the same time I know how much needs to be done before I could leave Longbourn… it is an intimidating concept. There are many farewell calls I will need to make, as well as all the preparations for moving."

"Would you prefer to wait, then?"

Elizabeth hesitantly asked, "Would you mind terribly if I did want to wait until after Jane's wedding?"

He gently kissed her hair. "My love, as long as you marry me, all else is unimportant."

"Thank you for understanding. So, Bingley could be willing to be imposed upon to delay their trip a week—perhaps we could accept that offer and marry just before they leave. It would need to be a small, simple service, but I am not sure I would not prefer that in any case."

"I would much prefer it that way, if I have a say in the matter. I have spent enough time dreading just standing up with Bingley."

She leaned her head back to look up at him in puzzlement. "Why would you dread that?"

"I always dread being in large gatherings of people—had you not noticed?"

Elizabeth shook her head as she took his words in.

"I always thought it must be embarrassingly obvious how I feel—I speak to no one, I attempt to stay as far away as

I decently can, I leave as soon as I can—I would rather be any place in the world, as long as there are fewer people there. I confess I am surprised you did not know."

Suddenly a good number of things began to make sense for Elizabeth. "I had noticed you kept somewhat apart, but I am afraid I quite misinterpreted it."

"Pray, how did you interpret it, then?" he asked with some amusement.

Elizabeth found she would really much rather not tell him that she had thought him exceedingly proud and disagreeable. "That is of no matter, now that I understand better."

"No, now I am curious as to what you were thinking, my sweet Elizabeth."

Elizabeth closed her eyes and gave a sigh. "I fear it does not reflect well on me, although I suppose it should be no surprise that I misconstrued yet one thing more about you. Very well, I thought you felt we were all beneath your notice."

Now it was Darcy's turn to look surprised. He said slowly, "I suppose it is little wonder, then, that you thought me so arrogant."

Hearing a degree of pain in his voice, she hastened to add, "But that was only when I first knew you. Your behavior at Pemberley showed me you were nothing of the sort, and I never saw any evidence of it in Kent, either, now that I think on it."

"You never saw me in a large gathering at Rosings or Pemberley. You may feel differently when you have." His voice was guarded.

She turned to face him. "I shall feel no differently at all," she said, and to punctuate her statement she raised her head and brushed her lips lightly against his.

As she withdrew, he immediately placed his hand behind her neck and drew her back to him for a much deeper, more lingering kiss. As they broke off, he said somewhat ruefully, "This may be a very long two weeks."

Elizabeth found herself with an unwontedly serious reaction to his comment. *In two weeks he will be my husband,* she thought. *In two weeks, we will be alone together and he will not stop with kisses.* She felt a peculiar lurch deep inside her at the thought of the unknown. Before Darcy could note her change in mood, she said lightly, "Patience is a virtue, Mr. Darcy."

"One I am afraid I do not possess when it comes to you, my dearest," he said. "But you still seem averse to calling me by my name, even when we are alone."

Elizabeth laughed. "And do you not know why, Mr. *Darcy?*"

"Please enlighten me."

She looked up at him through her lashes. "As you wish, Fitzwilliam."

A familiar light ignited in his eyes as he reached out to trace his finger across her lips and the line of her jaw. He smiled slightly as he shifted to allow her to lie in his arms. Elizabeth's breath caught as he slowly bent his head to capture her mouth. His tantalizing kisses distracted her from her purpose, and she gave in to the temptation to taste the pleasure he offered.

After a moment, though, she laid her fingers over his lips, and smiled mischievously up at him. "Do you still wish to know why I do not use your name? I have noted it seems to have a most peculiar effect on you, much as it just did. But I promise you, when we are safely married, I shall call you by it frequently."

He thoughtfully nibbled her fingertips, causing Elizabeth to feel a distinct loss of interest in discussing the matter any further. He noted to himself that it was true that, during the many times he had imagined her calling him by name, it was often in one very particular setting, with a particular response on his part. A slow smile came over his face. "You are a very wicked woman, Miss Bennet," he murmured. He began placing excruciatingly light and slow kisses on the soft, uncovered skin of her shoulder, while whispering, "Very, very wicked." By the time he had found his way to the sensitive hollow at the base of her neck, Elizabeth had given up any pretense of resistance, and allowed herself to tangle her fingers in his hair in encouragement. He continued to enjoy tantalizing her until her rapid breathing and arched body became too much for him, and their mouths met hungrily.

He lifted his face to allow her to meet his passion-darkened eyes. "Say my name, Elizabeth," he commanded softly. Shaking her head playfully, she attempted to pull his head back to hers. "Oh, no, Miss Bennet," he murmured. "No more kisses for you until you say it."

She raised her eyebrow. "I *am* very wicked," she said with a playful smile, and began reciting his name as rapidly as she could, with an inflection of mirth. With a mock glare, he nipped lightly at her neck, causing a squeal and fit of laughter. They smiled contentedly into one another's eyes, enjoying the game, until without warning the lighthearted moment shifted into a more serious one of deep attraction and desire.

Darcy slid one hand to her head, allowing his fingers to caress the silky curls he had longed to touch for so long. His thumb traced circles on her temple, and his breathing became shallow as he watched her eyes darken and her lips part. "Elizabeth," he whispered, making the syllables of her name into a caress.

"Fitzwilliam," she responded, her voice warm with passion. "Oh, Fitzwilliam."

It was far too close to his fantasies. He tried to assert control over his response, only to realize he had left it too long. He tasted her mouth, first lightly and then with burgeoning passion that stole away his senses. He knew that he must withdraw, but his lips would not cooperate and began to explore downward along her neck, then lower to the tender skin exposed by the neckline of her dress where he was not supposed to even allow his eyes to rest. He was even further inflamed by her gasps as this new sensation built in her to an excruciating tension.

Afterward Elizabeth would wonder what part of her had finally responded to her spiraling desire with a sense of panic that made her push him away. For a moment, Darcy looked at her uncomprehendingly as she withdrew from him, then he rose and took several rapid strides away from her. Facing away from her, he gripped one hand against a tree and stood in tense silence, staring unseeingly across the countryside.

Elizabeth also looked away, sobered by what had happened, and even more so by the realization of how far she had allowed her behavior to stray. How had it come to pass that she was allowing, nay, participating in the liberties he had taken? What was it about Darcy that tempted her to flout every rule she had ever known? She looked up to see him framed against the sunset, his unmoving form still in the attitude of painful tension. It hurt her to see him so, far more than she could explain to herself, and she realized the true question she should ask herself was how she came to love him so much that nothing else mattered.

"Mr. Darcy?" she said gently. Without turning, he held his hand up in a clear request that she desist. She bit her lip, not knowing how best to address his current distress, her own concerns forgotten in her apprehension for his. She waited briefly, then spoke his name again.

"Miss Bennet, please be so kind as to allow me to finish castigating myself before you take your turn; you may rest assured I am doing a very thorough job of it."

Hearing the bitterness of his words, she recognized what

she was witnessing was similar to Georgiana's description of another time when he failed to meet his own strict standards. She saw this was where she would need to begin thinking like a wife, for she would certainly need the capability to handle these situations in the future. Georgiana had indicated that offering sympathy was not productive, so a different approach was required. A thought occurred to her of how to draw him out of himself. "Perhaps what I am lacking, sir, is not an opportunity to castigate, but to receive comfort," she said.

He stiffened visibly, and for a moment Elizabeth thought her words had only served to make him blame himself yet further; then he approached her and, kneeling in front of her, took her hands in his. "Forgive me, my dearest; I was selfishly thinking only of myself, and not of you. Thank you for drawing my attention to the obvious."

She gave a slight smile. "Thank you for listening."

"Elizabeth, I shall always come when you ask, and no doubt more often than you would wish! Please do not distress yourself over what happened; it should not have happened, but given that it did, we can only remember that in two weeks we shall be man and wife, and none of this will matter."

She squeezed his hands. "It has been a rather emotional day, has it not?"

"Indeed," he agreed, "and I am sure that we are both somewhat overwrought at this point. I will not allow it to happen again."

"For two weeks."

"Yes," he said with a smile, "For two weeks. Then you must take your chances. But I note that the light is fading fast, and we should be returning to the house."

As he stood and moved to offer her his arm, she gave in to impulse and embraced him. In the circle of his arms, she thought to herself that perhaps her instincts would not serve her so ill with him after all.

Chapter 9

THE NEXT DAY PROVED to be just as busy as Elizabeth had anticipated, between a visit to the mantua-maker's shop in Meryton to select fabric and a model for her wedding gown, the arrival of the Gardiners and Jane, and the excitement of sharing her news. Darcy joined them for much of the day, and though Elizabeth felt the lack of time alone with him, she had the satisfaction of seeing her father taking pains to get acquainted with him. She was also pleased to notice Darcy in close conference with her uncle at one point. It was of great satisfaction to her to see their mutual respect.

That evening, after she retired, Elizabeth was not surprised to hear a knock on the door, as she had expected Jane would want to hear more about the recent events in private conversation. Her surmise was incorrect, however, in that her visitor was in fact Mrs. Gardiner.

"Lizzy, I wanted to tell you how very happy I am that you

and Mr. Darcy have reached an understanding," her aunt said warmly, taking her by the hands.

"Thank you. I had noticed you seemed to look with some favor on the idea," she replied. "But I must thank you for the little pushes you gave us in the right direction."

"My dear, that was my pleasure entirely. But as delightful as that subject is, I was hoping to have conference with you on a different matter."

Elizabeth, with some curiosity, invited her aunt to sit.

"The subject is somewhat delicate, and in many ways I feel Mr. Darcy should be telling you this himself, but he requested, I believe out of natural modesty, of your uncle that we be the ones to speak with you of this. He did not wish you to know of it earlier, but feels it is inappropriate to keep it a secret from you any longer, especially as some of the parties to the secret are not particularly trustworthy."

By this juncture, Elizabeth was burning with inquisitiveness and more than a little anxiety, wondering what could be so terrible that Darcy would be unwilling to tell her. "You are keeping me in suspense, aunt. What is this dread secret?"

Her aunt, however, seemed unable to be direct about the subject. "I told you, I believe, that Mr. Darcy called on us at Gracechurch Street several times after our return from Derbyshire, did I not? I did not, however, disclose the true purpose of his visits, which your uncle had, without my knowledge, been expecting from discussion with Mr. Darcy on our last day in Lambton. The first time he called, he was shut up with your uncle for several hours, and it was not until afterward that I learned that he had come to tell your uncle that he had found out where your sister Lydia and Mr. Wickham were, and that he had seen and talked with them both."

"He had done *what?*" Elizabeth asked, in utter astonishment.

"His goal was to secure and expedite their marriage. As you may have guessed, it was never Wickham's design to marry your sister, but he was in some rather serious financial straits, and was not proof against the temptation of immediate relief. Mr. Darcy met with him several times, as Wickham of course wanted more than he could get, but at length was reduced to be reasonable. After they had reached a settlement, Mr. Darcy acquainted your uncle with the situation, and then *they* spent some time battling out the question of who was to settle the matter. At last your uncle was forced to yield to Mr. Darcy's demand that nothing was to be done that he did not do himself, and agreed to his one request, which was that no one in your family be informed in any way of his part in this. This went sorely against the grain for both of us, but given how much we owed him, we did not deem it reasonable to refuse, though I will say it put me in quite a difficult position a few weeks later when you told me that Mr. Darcy would never be able to tolerate being in the same room as Wickham! And that, my dear, is the entire story."

Elizabeth's astonishment at this recounting was great, and

left her briefly speechless. Finally she asked, "But why did he not want me to know?"

"My dear, as I understand it, he was in hopes of winning your affections, and was concerned that if you knew of his role in this, you might accept him out of a sense of obligation, which was not his desire. I gather this is no longer a concern."

Elizabeth hardly knew what to think. That Darcy would have taken on himself all the trouble and mortification attendant on finding Wickham and Lydia, that he would agree to meet, reason with, persuade, and finally bribe, the man whom he always most wished to avoid, and whose very name it was punishment to him to pronounce—despite her high opinion of him, this went far beyond what she could have expected.

She had many more questions for her aunt, and the next hour was spent in conversation.

❧

The following day Elizabeth, knowing her chances of finding time alone with Darcy were slim, made a point of capturing him as soon as he arrived at Longbourn with Bingley, who was newly arrived at Netherfield. Drawing him off into the dining room, she took some time expressing her appreciation for all that he had done for Lydia and her pride in his actions. Darcy, who was less than comfortable with discussing the matter, made a concerted effort to change the subject, and eventually managed to work Elizabeth around to discussing wedding plans.

They resolved it would be best not to announce a date

for their wedding until after Jane and Bingley's was past, to avoid any explanation that might ruin Jane's honeymoon surprise. However, it seemed prudent to tell a few select people whose plans would be affected by their idea, and so Mr. Bennet, Georgiana, Bingley, and the Gardiners were informed. Mr. Bennet was not best pleased with the plan, since he was by no means ready to lose Elizabeth quite so soon, but he resolved to hold his peace after one look at Darcy's face when he suggested a delay.

Elizabeth did not in fact get a moment alone with Darcy until she saw him out of Longbourn when he prepared to depart that evening. Darcy, who had clearly been waiting for this opportunity the entire day, lost no time in finding a shadowy and secluded spot by the gate where he could pull her into his arms.

"Promise me you will reserve tomorrow afternoon for my *exclusive* use, or I will not be responsible for the consequences!" he whispered, feathering kisses behind her ear and down her neck.

"With or without chaperones?" asked Elizabeth, with what she thought to be remarkable aplomb given the sensations he was inducing in her.

"We seem to be rather troublesome for our chaperones. Perhaps we should not force anyone to struggle through the experience." He turned his attention to her hairline.

"You are very charitable, Mr. Darcy." Their mouths met in a hungry kiss that Elizabeth had been longing for all day.

When he released her, she leaned back against the wall and looked up at him. Darcy was breathing hard. "If *you* were charitable, Miss Bennet, you would marry me tomorrow," he said.

She pretended to consider the idea. "No, I'm afraid not. We would have to stay at Netherfield until Jane's wedding, and I do not plan to spend my wedding night as a guest in someone else's home."

She felt him stop breathing for a moment. He stepped toward her, and trapping her against the wall by placing his hands on either side of her, he said, "Miss Bennet, this is friendly advice which you can accept or disregard as you choose, but I would suggest that when you are alone in the dark with a man who is quite violently in love with you, it would be advisable to avoid mention of your wedding night."

She stood on her toes and proceeded to brush her lips against his unyielding ones tantalizingly until he could deny himself no longer and kissed her deeply. After a moment, she leaned back and said quite deliberately, "After all, I want you all to myself on our wedding night."

Darcy's hands gripped her arms tightly, but Elizabeth did not notice the discomfort. "I think you should go back to the house, Miss Bennet," he said with tight control.

She raised an eyebrow. "I fear that will not be possible, sir."

"Why is that?"

She glanced down at his hands with an amused smile. "Because you are not allowing me to, Mr. Darcy."

"Ah," he said, sounding surprised. "What a good idea of mine." He leaned forward, effectively pinning her against the wall, and proceeded to explore her mouth with a thoroughness and unrestrained passion that left her breathless. The exquisite sensation of his body against hers was augmented by the stirring feelings caused by his hands wandering down her arms and into the sensitive reaches of her back, caressing and demanding at the same time.

The temptation to touch him was more than she could control. She allowed her hands to explore the firm muscles of his shoulders, where, as if unsatisfied, they seemed to travel of their own accord inside the reaches of his coat and around his neck. The exhilarating feeling of his strength through nothing more than the thin cloth of his shirt left her weak.

"Elizabeth," he groaned. "What are you trying to do to me?" His kisses grew even more demanding as he pressed her closer to him.

Brought back to herself by his words, she drew her hands away, and removed temptation by concealing her face in his shoulder. He buried his face in her hair as he worked to regain control. "You seem to have moved from playing with fire to sitting on the volcano, my love," he said softly. "Please remember I am only too human."

"As I am well aware," she replied. "But you tempted me first, sir, by suggesting I might disregard your warning. I do not think I will believe you if you tell me that you were not hoping that I would say something provocative!"

"Caught again!" he exclaimed. "You are a dangerous woman, Miss Bennet." He stepped back from her and looked at her critically. "I would add that if you really do not wish to be married tomorrow, I suggest that you had best not meet your family until you have had a chance to repair some damage." He touched her hair lightly.

"I shall say good night then."

"Until tomorrow," he responded. Giving her one last look, he paused to trace his finger lightly along her collar-bone. "I hope you sleep better than I shall!" he said, and then was gone.

Two nights later, a large party assembled at Netherfield for the benefit of the many out-of-town guests arriving for the wedding. A number of neighborhood families were invited as well, including the Lucases and the Philips. Darcy chose to wait upstairs until the Bennets arrived along with Georgiana, who had surprised no one by choosing to remain at Longbourn until her return to town. He preferred to limit his exposure to the crowded scene, a sentiment which was reinforced by the knowledge Miss Bingley had been trying to corner him on his own ever since her arrival earlier that day. Finally the carriage he had been awaiting appeared, and his aspect changed to one of smiling anticipation.

He met the party at the door, offering one arm to Elizabeth and the other to Georgiana, who had received special permission to attend the gathering although she was not officially "out." Her excitement at the occasion was visible, contrasting with her brother who was quite ready to quit the assembly before he had even entered, and she was clearly more interested in enjoying the occasion with her friends than with her sedate older brother.

Darcy and Elizabeth drew a certain amount of attention from members of the assemblage due to the news of their engagement, and were thus required to circulate more than they might have chosen to otherwise. At one point, Darcy was drawn off by Bingley to converse with some mutual friends, and Elizabeth took the opportunity to search out Georgiana. She found her with Kitty, Mary, and some of their Meryton friends, in close conversation, which Elizabeth, glad to see her enjoying herself, chose not to interrupt. As she was returning to the main group, she chanced to hear her name spoken in a separate conversation by a familiar voice.

"Miss Eliza Bennet? A disappointment, to be sure, but not a fatal one." Miss Bingley's autocratic voice came clearly from the next room.

"You must be quite angry that she managed to allure him away from you," responded an unknown voice.

"I am not best pleased to lose Mr. Darcy's favor, it is true, but as for Miss Eliza, I feel mostly pity for the poor thing."

"Why would you pity her? She has made a brilliant match for herself—one has to wonder how she did it."

Miss Bingley sniffed. "I pity her because he will make her miserable. Oh, right now he is completely infatuated with the little chit, and will do absolutely anything to please her, even to the point of tolerating her abominable family. But will that be the case when the infatuation wears off? You know his pride—he may submerge it, but it will never disappear, and when he truly realizes what he has done, what sort of woman he has tied himself to, for whom he has been cut off by family and no doubt part of the *ton*, whom he has chosen to be a model for his sister—what will be the result then? She will be an embarrassment to him, and were her motives solely mercenary, this would no doubt be tolerable enough to her, but the poor thing clearly fancies herself in love with him. Indeed, I pity her for what will happen then, although a more sensible woman would have foreseen it and kept to her own level of society."

Elizabeth had overheard more than enough, and withdrew the way she had come to avoid detection. Her initial reaction was fury, but she soon converted herself back to humor as she realized that Miss Bingley's jealousy would not be able to let her engagement pass without any attempt at sabotage. There was bound to be talk of this sort when a woman of little fortune married a man of his wealth, and she needed to inure herself to the innuendoes. She reminded herself that, for all the relative brevity of their relationship, she knew Darcy far better than Miss Bingley did, and she knew the changes in his character were real ones. With that, she determined to seek him out again, and eventually found him cloistered in the library.

She smiled warmly at him. "Hiding away, my dearest?"

"Never from you." He stood, and, taking her hands in his, allowed his lips to brush lightly against hers. "Perhaps I was only waiting for you to find me so I might steal a few moments of your company to myself. Have I told you how very lovely you look tonight?"

"If you have, I give you permission to repeat yourself."

"As long as I may repeat this part as well." He leaned to kiss her again, with more passion this time. Elizabeth slid her arms around his neck and allowed herself to enjoy his kisses for several minutes, and then murmured, "Sir, we shall be missed."

"Let them miss us, then."

Elizabeth gave him a look which he could not misinterpret. Darcy sighed. "Once more unto the breach, then, my love?" he said, offering her his arm.

They returned in time to hear Mary and Georgiana take a turn at the pianoforte playing their newly learned Mozart duet, which was indeed lovely and received far warmer applause than Mary's usual performances. Both performers, flushed with pleasure, were immediately surrounded by friends praising their music. Darcy, amazed to see Georgiana performing in front of strangers in the first place, much less such a large assembly of them, determined to pay his compliments to her himself. They were somewhat delayed by Sir William Lucas, who felt a need to share his positive impressions of the event, though not without a necessary comparison to the Court of St. James. Elizabeth, who noted that Darcy was becoming increasingly taciturn as the evening progressed, made their excuses as quickly as possible.

Georgiana was in a circle of young people who were clearly enjoying themselves with substantially less dignity than their elders. Her hand resting lightly on the arm of a young man whom Elizabeth recognized vaguely as one of the Bingley cousins, she was laughing heartily at something Kitty was whispering in her ear.

Darcy's countenance changed. He stepped forward and drew Georgiana away from the others with a particularly hostile stare for the young man. She followed somewhat unwillingly. Elizabeth was able to hear only the beginning of the lecture Darcy was delivering with quiet anger to Georgiana, "Remember who you are and where you are!" Elizabeth bit her lip as she watched all the animation drain out of the girl's face. She made a whispered response, eyes on the floor, as her brother ended his scolding, and when he turned away, Elizabeth noted that she did not return to her friends, but instead looked around the room, and then approached Mrs. Gardiner and attached herself quietly to her.

Elizabeth had difficulty meeting Darcy's eyes when he returned to her, clearly still angered over Georgiana's behavior. She did not know how to comprehend his action, and he did not seem in a mood for explanations, yet she found herself roused to resentment on Georgiana's behalf, and saddened to see her behaving once again in her previous timid manner. "Mr. Darcy, it would seem that your sister took your words very much to heart," she said with a tinge of reproach in her voice.

He looked down at her coolly. "My sister and I understand each other quite well, Miss Bennet," he responded.

Taken aback by his tone, she said placatingly, "I am sure you do, although it is difficult for anyone to completely comprehend the sensitivity of a girl at that age."

"Sensitive she may be, but she is still a Darcy, and must behave appropriately. I will not have her behaving in such a manner," he said, glancing toward the group of young people.

Elizabeth felt her anger beginning to rise. "She did not seem to be behaving any differently from the rest of the young people."

As she pronounced these words, Mr. Darcy changed color. His voice became icy. "Miss Bennet, Georgiana will inhabit a different world than these people, and expectations for her will be different. What may seem completely normal to you may be regarded with the greatest of disapprobation in higher levels of society, and I will thank you to allow me to be the best judge of these matters."

"Indeed," Elizabeth said with quiet indignation, "how could I judge when my manners and breeding are no better than anyone else here, not including, of course, the Darcys!" In the back of her mind, she heard Miss Bingley's words again—*he may submerge his pride, but it will never disappear*—and she shuddered inwardly.

"Madam, I believe that we have covered this ground in some detail in the past! Georgiana's situation is different from yours, and that is all there is to it," he retorted.

"I see, and this would mean the very behavior you encourage in me would be unacceptable from her," she responded in a voice that was far too level.

He opened his mouth to respond, but said nothing, demonstrating clearly to Elizabeth his belief in the truth of her accusation. Finally he said, "I do not believe this is either the time or the place for this discussion, Miss Bennet!"

"You are quite right, sir. I believe that more than enough has been said. If you will excuse me." She turned and walked away swiftly, her composure close to breaking. She did not stop until she found herself on the outdoor terrace which, as the evening was turning chilly, was deserted. Wrapping her arms around herself against the cool air, she heard Miss Bingley's words in her mind again, and wondered whether she herself had been willfully blind, and so enchanted with Mr. Darcy as to mistake a superficial alteration in manners for a deeper change in perception.

Tears began to fall as she remembered the cold look he gave her. She reviewed his words in her mind, trying to find an alternate interpretation, and, finding none, attempting to find a justification. That she should not have tried to interfere in his discipline of Georgiana at this early stage in their relationship might be argued, as could the idea that she did not understand the expectations of the *ton*. Yet his attitude, his immediate rejection of her ideas, spoke much against him, as did the humiliation of not being held to the same standard as his sister.

My good opinion, once lost, is lost forever, his voice echoed from the past, and her tears began to flow in earnest as fear took its place in her heart. Had she, with a few ill-chosen words, lost his good opinion? The devastation this thought engendered in her went deeper than she would have believed possible. She attempted to reassure herself by reminding herself that she had said far worse things at Hunsford and been forgiven, but still a small part of her would not be comforted.

Shivering with cold, she struggled to determine what course she should take. The example of her parents had given her no insights into the resolution of quarrels. What advice would her aunt Gardiner give? She would advise speaking with him, but how, and where?

Her final question was answered for her as she realized that she was no longer alone. Darcy stood before her, and, taking his handkerchief, he began to gently dry her tears. Softly he said, "Elizabeth, you are quite right, and I am nothing but a hypocrite. I hold Georgiana to a standard I cannot meet, and no longer even want to meet, and it is not fair to her. Part of your appeal for me has always been your willingness to flout certain rules, and I would not have you alter that for the world."

His tenderness only caused her tears to flow more freely. "I must apologize for interfering between you and your sister, as well as for my intemperate words," she said, her voice shaking.

"Please do not; your point was a good one, and I count on you to help me understand Georgiana, as she is often a mystery to me. The truth is, it is past time for me to confess one of my greatest failings to you, and I can only hope for your under-standing and acceptance. I told you that I dread large gather-ings; that is only the beginning. I detest and despise them. I am never so uncomfortable as when I am in that setting, especially when I am forced to make conversation, and I find that I end up saying and doing things I would not in other circumstances, and later regret. In fact," he said with a slight smile, "I recall an assembly I once attended, where I said that a very lovely lady was not handsome enough to tempt me solely to avoid having to make conversation with a stranger."

"I… did not know. Thank you for telling me."

There was a long pause. Finally Darcy said, "Elizabeth, may I ask what you are thinking?"

"I was wondering much the same of you, in fact."

"If I tell you what I have been thinking, it will expose the full depth of my hypocrisy, since I would happily kill any man who said such a thing to Georgiana."

"You have whetted my curiosity, sir."

He stepped closer and put his mouth by her ear. "Elizabeth, I want nothing in the world so much as to kiss your tears away, and then to carry you upstairs and make you mine in every way," he whispered. "I want to bind you to me in every way I know, because I am terrified that you are going to tell me that you want nothing further to do with me."

Elizabeth put her arms around him. "I already am yours in every way, my dearest," she responded with tears in her eyes.

He crushed her to him and buried his face in her hair. "Elizabeth, my own Elizabeth," he murmured. "You mean everything to me. I could never bear it if you left me."

She tilted her head up and kissed him fiercely. "How could I ever leave you when I love you so much?"

He captured her mouth with his in a kiss of such passion that she felt its power run through her whole body, and she answered it with the deepest of ardor. He held her as tightly as he dared, as if she were his only surety in life, and the feeling of her soft body against him was almost more than he could bear. "You cannot imagine," he said between kisses, "how much I have longed to hear you say that you loved me."

"My dearest love, I shall say it until you tire of hearing it," she replied, every inch of her body responding to his touch and his fervent kisses. She wished she need never leave his embrace.

"Then you shall be saying it forever."

They heard the sound of a door opening behind them. Elizabeth tried to pull away, but Darcy held her still for one more deep kiss. "See how shameless I have become?" he whispered before he released her.

"Lizzy," her aunt's voice came softly. "It is time for us to leave. Perhaps you would like to say a quick good night to Mr. Darcy—I will be waiting just inside."

"Your aunt has my undying gratitude," Darcy whispered in her ear, pulling her to him again. "Now, where was I?"

Chapter 10

THE RIDE BACK TO Longbourn passed in a blur for Elizabeth. She was vaguely aware of Mrs. Bennet's ongoing raptures about the party and how lovely Jane had looked, and Mr. Bennet's frequent requests to hear less about it. She was still unsettled by her conversation with Darcy, and felt as if she had left part of herself behind at Netherfield.

The family retired immediately on their return to Longbourn, the hour being quite late, and Jane's wedding rehearsal scheduled for early the next morning. Elizabeth found herself too restless to think of sleep, and instead took a book into the drawing room in hopes of settling herself by reading. It was there that Mrs. Gardiner found her some time later, looking out the window into the darkness with the book lying closed in her lap. Elizabeth started guiltily at being caught woolgathering.

"My dear, you seem out of spirits this evening," her aunt said. "Is there anything I can do to help?"

Elizabeth smiled wryly. "It seems to be your burden this year to care for lovelorn nieces, does it not? First you had Jane this winter, then Lydia, and now me."

"Not to mention the occasional lovelorn future nephew. I have grown quite fond of your Mr. Darcy these last few months."

It was not the first time that Elizabeth had felt a pang of jealousy at the extent to which Darcy was using *her* aunt and uncle as confidantes. "I suppose it is only fair that he should turn to you, as it is quite impossible to imagine that he could turn to his own aunt for counsel in these matters!" She laughed as she pictured a tête-à-tête between Darcy and Lady Catherine de Bourgh.

"Well, I confess that it simplifies my life as an interfering aunt, my dear; if you refuse to tell me what is bothering you tonight, I can always ask him tomorrow."

"I shall save you the trouble, then, since nothing is in fact the matter, except that I find myself somewhat discomposed by my own feelings, and there is certainly no one I can blame for that but myself!"

"Are you upset with Mr. Darcy, then?"

"Not that; we did have a disagreement tonight, but we made our peace with one another afterward, yet I find myself still unsettled and uncertain of him, although he left me no reason at all to be uncertain. It is unreasonable, but it is even more unreasonable that I sit here, unable to sleep because I miss him so much, when I have just seen him and know full well that I will see him in the morning tomorrow and every day," Elizabeth said with a slight scowl of frustration.

"Love is rarely reasonable, my dear, especially the rather passionate kind of love that you and he seem to share. It sounds to me as if you are discovering just how necessary he has become to you, that even the shadow of a threat to his presence in your life frightens you."

"If this is love, how does anyone ever survive it, much less *want* to feel this way?"

"Well, Lizzy, it has been some years since I have had personal dealings with feelings of this intensity, since fortunately such feelings have a tendency over time to shift to quieter ones of trust and attachment. I believe, though, that you could take a few lessons from your young man, as he has perforce had to become something of an expert on surviving being in love."

Elizabeth exhaled slowly. "Aunt, this is not the first time that you have raised the subject of Mr. Darcy's sufferings on my account. I am beginning to think that you quite blame me for it!"

Mrs. Gardiner smiled, shaking her head. "Hardly, my dear. After all, you were completely entitled to refuse him, regardless of his feelings, but I have had an ongoing concern that you seem to underestimate the strength of his attachment to you. I am, in fact, rather glad to see you suffering just a bit in the name of love, since it tells me that your attachment to him may be becoming the equal of his for you; and though you are well matched in many ways, I have worried about an inequity in your regard for one another."

"Just because he had cared for me longer does not mean that my regard is any less than his!"

"Hush, Lizzy, I am not trying to start a competition; rather I hope to point out how similar your feelings sound to his. I rather suspect that his thoughts this evening are quite like yours."

Elizabeth considered this, and recognized that it was likely to be true, as she thought about his frequent half-jests about wishing to marry immediately, and she heard in her mind his words from earlier in the evening—*I want to bind you to me in every way I know, because I am terrified that you are going to tell me that you want nothing further to do with me.* No, their feelings were certainly quite similar, and she had an idea how best to give them both relief.

Darcy glanced at the clock and impatiently drummed his fingers on the arm of his chair. Bingley was never very punctual at the best of times, but surely the man could manage to be on time for the rehearsal for his own wedding! Not that he himself would have particularly cared about punctuality for the event were he not so anxious to see Elizabeth.

His night had been disturbed and restless after the previous day's events. No sooner had the Bennets' carriage pulled away the night before than he had commenced to brood about what Elizabeth might be thinking of his earlier behavior, and whether she would, on reflection, decide that she had forgiven him too quickly. Would she become angry again, or might she feel that she could not trust him? Accompanying these thoughts was the intense desire that her kisses had raised in him, and the combination was not conducive to a good night's sleep. Ending the night with his all too frequent dream of awakening with a loving Elizabeth in his arms did not help matters; although waking from his dreams was no longer the torture it had been in the months when he had felt no hope of ever bringing his desires to fruition, it was still wrenching to wake up alone. One definite benefit of married life, he decided, would be the possibility of a decent night's sleep again, preceded, of course, by passionate and tender lovemaking…

Enough of that, man! he chastised himself. With what certainly should have been the ease of long practice, given how often it had arisen, but in fact was an ongoing labor of Sisyphus, he pushed those thoughts away from the forefront of his mind. By the time Bingley finally appeared, Darcy was able to put aside his own worries long enough to exchange a few jests with him about his imminent loss of bachelorhood with good humor.

As they entered the church, his eyes immediately sought out Elizabeth. She had clearly been watching the door, and when she saw him, her eyes lit up with pleasure. With an inward sigh of relief that his worries had apparently been for naught, he approached her, automatically quelling the urge to take her in his arms, and instead allowed himself only to kiss her hand, and to stand a little closer to her than propriety dictated. She flushed slightly, and very appropriately cast her eyes down in response, but with a bewitching smile that reassured him as to her true reaction.

"Good morning, my sweetest Elizabeth," he said softly in her ear. "I trust you are well?"

"Very well, now," she replied, looking up at him with a tenderness that surprised him. "I missed you."

The urge to kiss her was becoming almost overwhelming, but since circumstances would not permit it, he could only murmur her name with longing, desirous to keep that affectionate look in her beautiful eyes as long as possible. Clearly able to divine his true wishes from the look on his face, Elizabeth smiled flirtatiously, making her look all the more kissable. Raising an eyebrow, he whispered, "If we were not standing ten feet from the parson, I would respond to that as it deserves."

Her gaze was warm as she said with the utmost gravity, "We certainly must not shock the parson."

"Not if you want to wait another week before we marry," he retorted good-humoredly.

To his surprise, she bit her lip and looked down. What had he done now to distress her? Finally, she looked up at him through her lashes and said tentatively, "Fitzwilliam?"

What had possessed her to call him by his name in this

setting? She was well aware—had pointed it out, in fact, with that astonishing perspicacity of hers—how viscerally he responded to the intimacy of her using his given name, and she accordingly restricted its use to moments of great physical closeness, of which this certainly did not qualify. What did she mean by it? For at least the thousandth time, he wondered whether she had any idea what a struggle it could be for him to be with her, to try to understand what she was thinking, not that he would give it up for anything in the world!

"Yes, Elizabeth," he answered, keeping his voice as carefully neutral as possible.

"I have been wondering whether it would be better not to wait so long as that."

Unable to credit that he had properly understood her, he asked, "You want to move the wedding day forward?"

"That… that is my thought, unless you would prefer not to do so."

What had happened? Until this point, he had been the one in a hurry to marry, and she had wanted to wait. "Elizabeth, I believe you know full well that nothing would make me happier than to marry you as soon as possible"—*preferably before this uncertainty drives me out of my mind*, he added to himself—"but will you allow me to ask why you suggest the change? Is it for my sake, or your own, or perhaps because you cannot trust our ability not to stray?"

She colored becomingly. "It is a bit of all three, although I must admit that my primary motives are selfish."

Did she have any idea of how he reacted when she said things like that? Unable to keep himself from touching her any longer, he cautiously and unobtrusively slipped his hand behind her and rested it on her lower back. With his thumb, he traced delicate circles over her spine, and smiled with satisfaction as he noted her response in the flushing of her cheeks and parted lips.

A trifle unsteadily, she said, "I must remind you that we are in church, sir."

His eyes locked with hers. "And I am doing my best to encourage you to enter into the state of *holy* matrimony as soon as possible."

"Lizzy!" Mrs. Bennet's piercing voice penetrated their private world. "You are needed! Oh, this is too vexing!"

They both started, and as Darcy finally took in their surroundings, he saw everyone's eyes on them, including a clearly amused Mr. Bennet.

The parson coughed, and began to explain to Elizabeth her role in the ceremony, allowing Darcy a few moments to collect himself before receiving his own set of instructions, as if he could concentrate on anything else after Elizabeth's words. He struggled to contain his impatience as they walked through the stages of the service. As soon as she took her position across from him, he caught her eye and mouthed the question, "When?"

She glanced around, and seeing everyone's attention focused elsewhere, and allowed her lips to shape the word, "Friday."

His heart pounded. Friday was only three days away—she could be his so soon! Intoxicated by the concept, he countered soundlessly, "Thursday."

The corners of her mouth twitched, but she shook her head slightly. "Friday," she insisted silently.

He smiled slowly in return. "Thursday."

"If I could have the *complete* attention of the bridesmaid and the groomsman for just a few minutes," the parson said with some acerbity. Elizabeth, looking guilty, turned her attention forward.

Darcy continued to watch her, attending only slightly to the proceedings. At first he was content to bask in her presence and the knowledge that she wanted to marry so soon, but as she continued to avoid meeting his eyes, he began to wonder if she thought he had been too forward for suggesting an even earlier date. It seemed unlikely, as he had certainly made similar proposals to her in the past few days with no ill effect, so perhaps this was another case of his worrying over nothing. But perhaps it was not—he cast a searching gaze over Elizabeth, hunting vainly for some hint as to her state of mind.

He wondered if he would ever gain a sense of certainty about her feelings for him, or if his life was to be a continual cycle of worrying that he had somehow offended her. Surely marriage would help, and time would allow him to rebuild the sense of confidence that had been shattered at Hunsford. He had misread her so badly before that, and her change of sentiment toward him at Pemberley had happened so rapidly; how was he to feel certain of her?

When the rehearsal drew to a close, and the party prepared to adjourn to Longbourn, he finally managed to catch her attention. "Will you walk out with me, Elizabeth? It seems we have much to discuss."

She hesitated, clearly torn between a desire to be alone with him and wondering about the wisdom of such a course, given their history.

"I will even promise to make an attempt to behave, if that will help," he said.

"To make an attempt to behave? Does that mean that you do not usually make such an attempt, sir?" she responded playfully.

"Perhaps it means that I frequently encounter provocation beyond the ability of man to ignore," he retorted in like spirit.

She shook her head with mock gravity. "Clearly I have misconstrued you yet again; it had seemed to me that you enjoyed being so provoked, sir."

With a slow smile, he said, "You know very well what I like, my dearest, and at the moment I believe *you* would like to see how quickly you can defeat my resolve!"

Elizabeth glanced up at him, and gave a dramatic sigh. "Then I suppose that I must try not to say anything too provocative, since you clearly understand me too well!"

Darcy could not help but laugh. "Do not stop for my sake,

my love! But to the subject at hand, please forgive my impatience earlier. If Friday is what you wish, Friday it shall be."

With a teasing look, she responded, "Whereas I was beginning to think that a case could be made for Thursday! Sir, I must conclude that you and I are in danger of becoming altogether too agreeable."

He laid a hand on her arm. "You are not angry, then?"

She looked at him in surprise. "Not in the slightest! If I have some cause for anger, I remain blissfully unaware of it."

He smiled with relief—another false alarm. "When you would not look at me in the church, I was concerned. I am glad to know that it was groundless."

Elizabeth laughed. "I was *trying* to pay attention to the rehearsal!"

"Whereas I myself have long since given up on paying attention to anything else when you are present!" His gaze warmed. "I recall once, last November, when you came into the library at Netherfield while I was reading there. You selected a book to read—some Renaissance poetry, if I am not mistaken—and I recall spending fully half an hour concentrating on turning the pages of my book at appropriate intervals so that you would not discover how much your presence distracted me."

"You were quite successful, then, as I was typically oblivious to any of it!" said Elizabeth with some chagrin. "Even then, so early in our acquaintance, you had noticed me?"

"It took me very little time to notice you, but a great deal of time making an effort *not* to notice you."

"You fought it so? When, then, did you begin to love me? I can comprehend your going on charmingly when you had once made a beginning, but what set you off in the first place?"

"I cannot fix on the hour, or the spot, or the look, or the words which laid the foundation. It is too long ago. I was in the middle before I knew I had begun. Can you name the moment when you first realized that you loved me?"

"Easily—it was in Lambton, at the inn; I had just told you of Lydia's folly. You said you were leaving, and I assumed that you wanted to avoid any further association with me. I thought that I should never see you again, and that was when I knew that I loved you."

"You should have known by then that you could not be rid of me so easily!"

"Please recall that I had, at that point, hardly begun to reassure myself that you still cared for me at all! I am almost afraid of asking what you thought of me, when we met at Pemberley."

"I felt nothing but surprise at first. Well, in truth, my very first thought was that I had somehow conjured you up from thin air, since you had been very much in my mind all that day."

"As you had been in mine, but I had the excuse of being at your home, and hearing about you from your housekeeper. But why were you thinking of me?"

He took her hand and looked at it gravely. "You would no

doubt be startled, my love, to know how frequently you were in my mind then." He paused, remembering that afternoon, and his decision to reach Pemberley a day before the remainder of the party in order to have the opportunity to privately exorcise Elizabeth's ghost from his home. It was the first time he had been there since Kent, and he had spent so many hours imagining her by his side there that he knew his return would be a painful reminder of the fact she would never be his. Finally clearing his head from the constant refrain of *she has never been here; she never will be here* during his ride to Pemberley, and then almost the minute he dismounted, he discovered that she *was* there.

He thought with mortification of the figure he must have cut then, covered with road dust and no doubt stinking of horse. "When I came across you there I was certainly at my least presentable, not only in appearance but in my complete inability to hold a coherent conversation—and what did you think, seeing me so?"

Elizabeth colored and laughed. "I was far too preoccupied with my own embarrassment to give a thought to your position! I thought you would believe I was throwing myself in your path, and I certainly did not expect any consideration from you at all!" She paused, then added, "But I must admit I did notice how handsome you looked."

"That, my dearest, sounded suspiciously like a provoking comment! But back to the past, before my resolve weakens, I have often wondered about the letter I wrote you—did it soon make you think better of me? Did you, on reading it, give any credit to its contents?"

"At first reading, I tried to dismiss it all as falsehood, but almost immediately I recognized the justice of some of your points, especially as regarded Wickham. I grew absolutely ashamed of myself, I, who had been so certain of my perceptions; and I bitterly regretted the accusations I had made to you. It took somewhat longer for me to admit that your role in separating Bingley from Jane, while unsupportable from my point of view, was at least capable of a different interpretation than I had given it. I had already realized, even before receiving your letter, how poorly I had treated you; that, in presenting me with the compliment of your affections, you deserved at least politeness from me."

"Perhaps if I had been more polite and respectful toward you, that would have been true, but as it is, I deserved the full measure of your anger for my behavior that night."

"You came in for more than your share of it, sir, since you unknowingly presented your proposal at a time when I was already fully exasperated with you. Colonel Fitzwilliam, only that afternoon, had let slip something which confirmed your role in Bingley's decampment from Netherfield, and I was quite preoccupied with that when you arrived."

"While I, in my abominable pride, believed you to be wishing, expecting my addresses. Can you believe my vanity?" he said with a remorseful smile, and kissed the palm of her hand.

Elizabeth laughed lightly. "I can believe it quite well,

since it was not so many months until I was indeed wishing for your addresses! I have often wondered if, had I recognized your inclination earlier, I would have been able to look beyond my prejudices to find the good in you sooner."

"Elizabeth," Darcy said with great seriousness, "you did me the greatest of favors in refusing my first proposal. Not only did you teach me a much needed lesson about how my behavior looked to the world, but it also allowed me the very great privilege and joy of knowing that you have now accepted me out of affection, not merely for the place I could offer in society, which is why I expected your acceptance then. I would not be deprived of that for the world, my love."

He wondered if she realized just how vulnerable he felt when he told her of his feelings and her importance to him, and he leaned over and kissed her tenderly in search of that reassurance he could find only in her touch.

She put her hand lightly to his face and said, "Since I would not be deprived of *you* for the world, I must thank you for allowing us a second chance after my behavior in Kent."

"How could I have let you go, once I saw you again?"

Their lips met again, and Elizabeth closed her eyes to further savor the exquisite sensation that ran through her. She could feel Darcy's attempt to restrain himself, and all too soon he pulled away, leaving her still hungry for his touch. She was slightly comforted to discover that his breathing was somewhat ragged as well.

"Elizabeth, may I ask you a question?"

"You seem to have done so several times in the last few minutes, and I do not believe I have objected so far!" she teased.

He lifted a hand to cup her cheek. "You never actually answered me when I asked why you wished to move the wedding forward," he said, his gaze intent on her.

Elizabeth felt her breath coming more quickly. "Oh, dear. How precisely am I to answer that without being provocative, Mr. Darcy?"

His eyes darkened, and he allowed his fingers to trail along the line of her jaw. "You managed to use my name perfectly well in church earlier, my love."

"Who is being provocative now?" Elizabeth struggled to keep her voice from trembling as she involuntarily responded to his touch.

"Should I stop?" His lips caressed her neck, then moved agonizingly slowly to the tender skin below her ear. She clutched at his shoulders for support. "Elizabeth?"

She felt his need echoing her own and, hearing the plea for permission in his voice, shuddered as his arms came around her. "Do not stop," she said huskily into his ear. "Please do not stop."

Giving up any vestige of control, he pulled her to him, and she rejoiced in the feeling of his body against hers. She moaned his name, further kindling his need, and his mouth met hers with a fiery passion that stirred her deeply. His hands on her back encouraged her to press herself against him, and she felt every inch of her body crying out for his touch.

How long they lost themselves in each other's arms was unclear; Elizabeth only knew that it ended too soon, and she found herself leaning against his shoulder. "So much for behaving," she said shakily.

"So much for not being provocative!"

"What do you mean? I was quite careful not to say anything provocative!" she cried.

He laughed. "Do you not know how much you provoke me simply by being near me, looking at me, smiling at me?"

"I believe that I am being held to an impossible standard!" she teased.

"Leaving me in an impossible position, madam, which is why I favor making you my wife as soon as possible."

She leaned back and met his eyes. Raising an eyebrow, she said, "Thursday, then?"

He smiled. "I believe that I can survive until then, given an adequate number of kisses to keep me going."

"And what, pray tell, would be an adequate number, sir?"

He paused as if to consider, reveling in the sense of freedom and lightness that he experienced only in her arms. "I will tell you when you we get to it," he said, suiting his actions to his words by recapturing her mouth. "But I hope you were not planning on getting home soon."

Chapter 11

IT WAS RESOLVED BETWEEN them that Darcy would approach the parson regarding performing the wedding, and Elizabeth would attend to the details of the actual ceremony. The burden of this was much reduced by Mrs. Gardiner, who, as soon as she heard of the revised plan, offered her services in organizing the event. "I shall quite enjoy it, my dear, and you are making it so very simple by keeping things quite small. We need no rehearsal, as we are all *quite* in practice on weddings, and I am certain that I will need only mention the prospect to your cook, as she is still so offended that Jane's wedding breakfast is to be held at Netherfield that I am sure she will produce a veritable feast!"

Elizabeth was all gratitude for the assistance, for she had discovered to her chagrin that her early feelings of relief after scheduling the wedding were rapidly being superseded by mounting anxiety and uneasiness, though precisely about what she was not entirely certain. She found herself becoming almost uncivil, and developed a sudden sympathy with Mrs. Bennet's fits of nerves. She began to feel the chief advantage of the changed wedding date was that it would be done with that much sooner, and was glad to escape from company when it finally came time to retire for the evening.

It was long past midnight when she awoke in panic from a nightmare. *She was back at Hunsford with Darcy, only this time, she was the one confessing her love to him, and he was rejecting her in the strongest possible terms, stating his dislike, demeaning her very character, refusing to grant even the smallest degree of warmth. Her devastation was complete...* She pressed her hand against her mouth, tears running down her face. It was only a dream, she told herself firmly, but she continued to tremble. She was not accustomed to allowing herself to be vulnerable to the opinions of others; although she had the facility for making friends easily, she could also part with them with much of the same ease, and her wit provided an easy defense against most forms of criticism. Nothing had prepared her for the deep-seated need she felt for Darcy's affection, and it alarmed her.

She reached for a handkerchief to dry her tears, and as she raised it to her face, discovered it to be the long-cherished one of Darcy's, reclaimed from its exile in her father's desk, but never returned to its rightful owner. She found herself clutching it for comfort, much as she had in the days when she was most uncertain of his regard.

Hunsford… how could she ever have justified her behavior that day? She could see now he had come to her that day with this same sense of need and vulnerability, and she had completely failed to recognize it. He had even tried to express it in his own unfortunate way by telling her the great obstacles his feelings had to overcome before he could make her his offer, but his proud words about the inferiority of her own state and her connections blinded her to anything else.

Her words came back to haunt her—*From the very beginning, from the first moment I may almost say, of my acquaintance with you, your manners impressing me with the fullest belief of your arrogance, your conceit, and your selfish disdain of the feelings of others, were such as to form the ground-work of disapprobation, on which succeeding events have built so immovable a dislike; and I had not known you a month before I felt that you were the last man in the world whom I could ever be prevailed on to marry.* She shuddered to think of the pain she must have caused him. With her newfound insight into the depths of her love for him, she recognized for the first time that, in addition to the misjudgment of him which she had long since acknowledged, she was also guilty of a great cruelty, with her only excuse being a lack of understanding for which she could no longer forgive herself.

And yet he had forgiven her, and even her pitiless words could not keep him from writing that memorable adieu in his letter the next day—*I will only add, God bless you.* He had changed his manners since then, but, as she had once noted to Wickham, he had never changed in the essentials—his fierce loyalties, his love for his family and his home, his disdain for any sort of deceit, his quick mind, his formidable standards for his own behavior. *Love is certainly a humbling experience*, she thought. *I hope it becomes easier with time*.

⚜

"Dearly beloved, we are gathered together here in the sight of God, and in the face of this congregation, to join together this Man and this Woman in holy matrimony; which is an honorable estate, instituted of God in the time of man's innocency, signifying unto us the mystical union that is betwixt Christ and his Church; which holy estate Christ adorned and beautified with his presence, and first miracle that he wrought, in Cana of Galilee; and is commended of Saint Paul to be honorable among all men: and therefore is not by any to be enterprised, nor taken in hand, unadvisedly, lightly, or wantonly, to satisfy men's carnal lusts and appetites, like brute beasts that have no understanding; but reverently, discreetly, advisedly, soberly, and in the fear of God; duly considering the causes for which matrimony was ordained."

The familiar words of the wedding service washed over Elizabeth as she stood next to Jane, who was as radiant as any bride could be. She was fully determined to enjoy the occasion, regardless of her earlier frame of mind. She tried to listen thoughtfully, contemplating her own state, but her thoughts kept slipping away. For once she could not blame

Darcy for her inattentiveness, since he, for the most part, was looking at no object but the ground. A slight smile of affection came to her lips as she watched him; she knew how greatly he had been dreading standing up in front of this great crowd of people, and she took no offense at his withdrawn behavior, but only wished she could send some comfort to him from across the aisle. Even as she thought this, he raised his eyes to her.

"Wilt thou have this woman to thy wedded wife, to live together after God's ordinance in the holy estate of matrimony? Wilt thou love her, comfort her, honor, and keep her in sickness and in health; and, forsaking all other, keep thee only unto her, so long as ye both shall live?"

Bingley's firm response, "I will," echoed throughout the church.

Elizabeth's gaze remained caught by Darcy's as Jane's turn came.

"Wilt thou have this man to thy wedded husband, to live together after God's ordinance in the holy estate of matrimony? Wilt thou obey him, and serve him, love, honor, and keep him in sickness and in health; and, forsaking all other, keep thee only unto him, so long as ye both shall live?"

"I will," responded Jane in a tremulous voice.

Elizabeth's heart skipped a beat as she thought of saying those same words the following day, and all they implied. Darcy's steadfast gaze comforted her, reminding her he would be with her, and that their separations were coming to an end. She lost herself in contemplation of their future, nearly missing her cues in the ceremony, and was glad when she could finally take Darcy's arm to follow Jane and Bingley from the altar.

❦

"Well," said Mrs. Bennet, as soon as the family settled themselves at Longbourn after the wedding breakfast, "what say you to the day? I think everything has passed off uncommonly well, I assure you. As for my dear Jane, I never saw her look in greater beauty."

"It went very well indeed," agreed Mrs. Gardiner. "It was a testament to your fine planning, Mrs. Bennet."

Mrs. Bennet, who was in very great spirits, was not to be suppressed. "Next it shall be your turn, my dear Lizzy! We must begin our planning soon—there is so much we must do!"

Darcy glanced at Elizabeth, who was feeling uncommonly anxious about the discussion, well aware that her mother would take her news neither well nor with dignity.

"Well, we have not wished to distract you in any way from your planning from Jane's wedding, knowing how much depended on you," Elizabeth temporized. "We have been proceeding with our own planning in the meantime, however."

"Without any input from me? I see no reason you could not have waited!"

Elizabeth cast a helpless look at Mrs. Gardiner. "We

could not wait because we plan to marry very soon, in fact, tomorrow," she said, bracing herself. She wished that Darcy were not present to see the mortifying explosion that was sure to come.

"Nonsense, nonsense! Lizzy, I swear you delight in vexing me! I know you must be teasing me!"

Darcy decided it was time to come to Elizabeth's rescue. "I assure you she is doing nothing of the sort, madam. We will be married tomorrow; the plans have been set," he said in a voice that brooked no argument. Elizabeth glanced at him gratefully.

Mrs. Bennet, who was still sufficiently in awe of her future son-in-law to be taken aback, especially when he spoke in such a manner, said weakly, "But... your trousseau, you cannot be married without your trousseau! Oh, Lord! And there are many guests to invite, and planning..."

"We want only the immediate family present, and, as we will be going to London directly after the wedding, I can address the question of a trousseau then," Elizabeth said placatingly.

"You cannot do that after the wedding! It must be before, it must! Oh, you have no compassion for my nerves, Lizzy!" Mrs. Bennet turned to her husband, whose attention was deep in a book, and cried, "Oh! Mr. Bennet, you must help me! Lizzy wants to marry Mr. Darcy tomorrow! You must make her change her mind!"

Mr. Bennet raised his eyes from his book, and fixed them on her face with a calm unconcern which was not in the least altered by her communication. "My dear, I thought that you wanted Lizzy to marry Mr. Darcy."

"You are trying to vex me! I do not want them to marry tomorrow!"

"Well, I cannot see why they should not. I am perfectly at leisure tomorrow."

"Mr. Bennet! How can you allow this?"

"My dear, it would seem to me that if two young people insist on marrying in a hurry, perhaps it is best not to question too deeply. Now, madam, I shall be in my library where I may be assured of some peace."

As Mr. Bennet retreated, Georgiana and Kitty were doing their best to stifle giggles, Mary looked disapproving, and Elizabeth was biting her lip in an attempt to disguise a smile. Darcy, less willing to be the subject of this kind of humor, especially in front of his sister, said, "Mrs. Bennet, may I speak with you privately for a moment?" He sent an amused glance to Elizabeth as he ushered her mother out of the room.

"Mrs. Bennet," he began in a severe manner, every inch the Master of Pemberley. "I fear you may be subject to some misunderstanding on this matter. The decision on the date was mine. I am not a patient man, and your daughter has kept me waiting a very long time, and I have no intention of waiting any longer. The frank truth is that it is tomorrow or Gretna Green. Do I make myself quite clear?"

Looking most flustered, Mrs. Bennet said, "Of course, Mr. Darcy... I am sorry if I... it is only that Lizzy can be so headstrong at times, and I thought… pray forgive me, but I had assumed that you would want a more proper wedding, but you prefer this… of course, as you wish!"

With a gleam in his eye that Elizabeth would have recognized instantly, he responded, "Had your daughter seen fit to accept me last April, matters might have been arranged differently, but, as you say, she can be quite headstrong."

Mrs. Bennet's eyes grew wide, and she said faintly, "Last April… Lizzy… I cannot understand…"

"Well, madam, I am glad that we understand one another. Shall we return to the company?"

As Darcy held the door for her, he shot Elizabeth a triumphant look over Mrs. Bennet's head. "Well, now that we are all in agreement, are there any other matters that must be addressed?"

Mrs. Gardiner, seeing the stunned look on her sister-in-law's face, determined that the time had come for some soothing of nerves. "My dear Mrs. Bennet, I hope that you will not think this *too* presumptuous of me, but in my concern for the *many* demands placed on you this week, I took the liberty of speaking with your cook myself about the wedding breakfast. I know she is *most* anxious to go over the arrangements with you, and perhaps this would be a good time." She gently steered Mrs. Bennet from the room.

Elizabeth eyed Darcy with some suspicion, but also with pride for his confident handling of her mother. "What did you say to her?"

He glanced significantly at the corner where Georgiana, Mary, and Kitty sat. "We discussed our points of view."

Kitty whispered something in Georgiana's ear, then, with a look which indicated she thought them both spoilsports, said, "I can tell when we are not wanted." She swept out of the room, followed closely by the other two girls.

Mr. Gardiner also stood and made to join the exodus. "I think it must be time for me to take my leave as well, unless you want a chaperone," he said, with a twinkle in his eye. Elizabeth, smiling, shook her head, and he departed.

She stared at Darcy expectantly. He said, "I told her that it was tomorrow or Gretna Green."

"But that is completely ridiculous. You would never elope!"

"You know that, as do I, but I doubt your mother is sensible of it! Also, I gave her something else to worry about as a distraction."

"What do you mean?"

He smiled teasingly. "I told her you had refused me in April. She may never forgive you."

"I'm sure she will not!" cried Elizabeth feelingly. "It is a good thing for my safety that we will be departing tomorrow!"

"It is a good thing for my peace of mind, that much is for certain!" He took her hand and pressed a light but lingering kiss in her palm.

Elizabeth, distracted by the exquisite sensation his casual gesture produced in her, attempted to look composed, but Darcy's observant eyes did not miss her reaction. With a slight smile, he repeated his action, then continued his atten-tion by touching his lips lightly to the sensitive skin inside her wrist. His gaze growing intent, he murmured, "You may have dismissed your uncle too soon, my dearest, for I fear you may have need of a chaperone after all."

"His question was not if I *needed* a chaperone; but whether I *wanted* one," she said demurely.

His smile grew. "I see we are back to provocative remarks."

"Is that a complaint, sir?"

"Not at all," he said, punctuating each word with another kiss inside her captive hand. He turned his attention to her fingers one at a time, never taking his eyes off her. Elizabeth, astonished by the degree of pleasure she was deriving merely from the touch of his lips on her hand, leaned toward him, expectant that he would kiss her, but Darcy, with a glint in his eye, continued his tantalizing exploration until she shivered visibly in response. He moved nearer and finally answered her need by capturing her lips with his own, and, taking advantage of the moment of distraction as his desire met hers, drew her toward him and into his arms.

She said, "Fitzwilliam, if someone walks in..."

"They will be very shocked," he completed her sentence, his lips exploring the angles of her face. "Elizabeth, my love, tomorrow you will be my wife."

Torn between anxiety that they would be discovered and her hunger for his touch, she hesitated until at last his mouth met hers again and any remaining rational thought fled her mind. The intoxicating feeling of his hands pressing her close to him made her tremble as she lost herself in the pleasure of his kisses. Fortunately, no one did walk in.

Chapter 12

W<small>HEN THE GENTLEMEN RETIRED</small> for port after dinner, Mrs. Bennet was left to hold forth at length to the ladies about the plans for Elizabeth's wedding. This was more tolerable to her daughter than it might have been otherwise, since it was her first opportunity to hear from Mrs. Gardiner what plans had been made. Mary was to assist Elizabeth in her preparations, since Jane would not arrive until the actual time of the ceremony; while Kitty and Georgiana were to gather the last flowers of the season to decorate the church early in the morning. Georgiana, to no one's great surprise, had accepted an invitation to remain at Longbourn for an additional week before returning to London in order to give the newlyweds some privacy.

A knock was heard at the front door, and a few moments later, Hill entered the drawing room. "There is a *gentleman* to see Miss Elizabeth," she announced, managing to imply through her tone that no unknown man who called so late in the day could truly be deemed a gentleman. Curious, Elizabeth bade her to show him in, and shortly after, Hill announced the mysterious gentleman.

"Colonel Fitzwilliam!" cried Elizabeth. "This is indeed a surprise!"

"As was the express I received yesterday from Darcy, I assure you," he responded. "It is most delightful to see you again, Miss Bennet." He spotted Georgiana and, with an expression of surprise, greeted her with a kiss on the cheek.

Elizabeth introduced the colonel to her mother, sisters, and aunt, and asked Hill to request that Mr. Darcy join them at his earliest convenience.

"So he *is* here," said Colonel Fitzwilliam. "I must apologize for the hour of my call, but when I presented myself at Netherfield looking for my cousin, I was told in no uncertain terms by the servants that not only was Darcy absent, but that Bingley was not receiving guests since it was his wedding day. Since you, Miss Bennet, are the sole acquaintance I can claim in Hertfordshire apart from Bingley and Darcy, I decided to throw myself on your mercy in hopes that you could direct me to my cousin, and the Netherfield staff were so kind as to provide me an escort here."

"Very wise, Colonel," laughed Elizabeth. "It is certainly the case that Mr. Darcy is generally here if he is not at Netherfield, and we are all avoiding Netherfield today! But please, will you join us? I would imagine you would be in need of some refreshment after your journey—have you come from London?"

"Yes, fortunately I was in town to receive the post. So, I understand I must offer you my felicitations, Miss Bennet. I must say that Darcy has been more sly than usual; I admit that I had no inkling that the wind was blowing in this direction."

At that moment, Darcy himself entered and greeted his cousin heartily. "So you did make it, Fitzwilliam," he said, "I doubted you would be able to come on such short notice."

"Well, it is traditional to give more than one day's notice on a wedding invitation," said Colonel Fitzwilliam with a laugh. "You should have heard my mother on the subject!"

"I am just as happy I did not," said Darcy dryly. "Sometimes it is best to hope for forgiveness after the fact."

"Well, Father was quite entertained, I must say—he said immediately, 'Well, we know where he gets that from. I don't want to be the one to tell Catherine, though.'" His imitation brought a delighted smile to Georgiana's face.

"So, Mr. Darcy, where *do* you get that from?" asked Elizabeth archly.

"I see no reason to dredge up old family stories for you until we are actually married, my dear," said Darcy austerely, "no matter how much my cousin chooses to embarrass me."

"Well, I shall take pity on you, Miss Bennet," said Colonel Fitzwilliam. "Let me just say that his father was known for his, um, forthrightness and persistence in his court-ship of my aunt."

"I see," said Elizabeth with a sparkle in her eyes. "I shall look forward to hearing the full story someday."

The conversation continued in this vein for some time, until the colonel remarked, "Well, I am sure it is past time for me to take my leave. Darcy, I wonder if you would be so kind as to direct me to a nearby inn. I confess that I had planned to throw myself on Bingley's mercy for the night, but under the circumstances, I believe I should make other arrangements."

Elizabeth cast a significant look at her mother, who, quite overwhelmed by having the son of an earl in her home, had said barely a word. Thus prodded, Mrs. Bennet said, "Oh, Colonel Fitzwilliam, there is no need for that! The inn at Meryton is hardly suitable for a gentleman such as yourself. We would be most honored if you would consent to stay here."

Colonel Fitzwilliam looked at her in surprise. "That is a most gracious offer, madam, but I am well aware that, with your daughter's wedding tomorrow, you must have quite enough without a guest, as well," he said courteously.

Mr. Bennet said dryly, "Although it is true that we have a wedding tomorrow, it is hardly an unusual burden; we marry off daughters nearly every day here—Jane today, Lizzy tomorrow, and I am certain that Kitty or Mary will have found someone by the end of the week. So you can see, sir, it will not put us out in the least."

Colonel Fitzwilliam looked puzzled, and Elizabeth took mercy on him. "Mr. Bingley's bride is my eldest sister, Colonel Fitzwilliam, so you see that it is indeed quite a week for weddings here." A look of understanding passed over his face, followed immediately by a quickly veiled doubtful look directed first at Darcy, then at Elizabeth. Clearly he recalled all too well Darcy's confidences about Bingley, and was drawing some interesting conclusions.

"Indeed, Colonel Fitzwilliam, it would be no trouble. As you can see, we already have the Gardiners and Georgiana as houseguests, and one more would make little difference," said Elizabeth warmly.

"Yes, do stay," Georgiana added. "I have so much to tell you about!"

"In that case, I gratefully accept your offer of hospitality, Mrs. Bennet," he said.

The addition of Colonel Fitzwilliam to the party added a certain liveliness; he entered into the conversation directly and talked very pleasantly. Elizabeth found she enjoyed his company as much as she had in Kent, and she was pleased to see Georgiana was well entertained as well. Kitty was clearly quite taken with his manners and demeanor, and indulged herself in the occasional fluttering of eyelashes in his direction, though, fortunately, without the blatancy that characterized her behavior when the regiment was in Meryton. The colonel had a well-informed mind which allowed him to challenge Mr. Bennet to a degree that intrigued the latter, who for once chose to remain in company rather than retreat to his library.

It was not until near suppertime that Elizabeth noticed

that Darcy was not contributing to the conversation. At first she thought the party had grown too large for his taste, but as she continued to observe him, she began to suspect he was actively displeased. Perhaps the invitation Mrs. Bennet had extended in all civility made him unhappy; she could well understand that he might prefer to limit his cousin's exposure to the Bennet household. She could feel the tension radiating from him, and could think of no other cause. With concern, she redoubled her efforts at amiability toward Colonel Fitzwilliam, hoping to alleviate Darcy's anxiety over what his cousin might think, but his grim looks continued unabated, and the responses he made were as brief as civility would permit.

When Darcy finally deemed it late enough for him to return to Netherfield without risk of disturbing the newlyweds, he asked Elizabeth to walk him out. Noting he still had a forbidding set to his mouth, she put a hand on his arm as soon as they were beyond the lights of the house. To her surprise, he gathered her tightly into his arms without any of his usual preliminaries and kissed her with fierce demand. Elizabeth was at first taken aback by his approach, but the intensity of his ardor soon stirred an equal need in her, and she matched his desperate possessiveness as she sought her own satisfaction from his lips. His grip on her bespoke a more violent and uncontrolled passion than was common for him, but, instead of frightening her, it seemed to tap into a well of desire she had never known existed, and a hunger which could not be quenched.

Intoxicated by his urgent kisses, she pressed herself against him as if she could never get close enough. Finally he broke off as abruptly as he had begun, and she clung to his shoulders, feeling dizzy from her response to his forceful passion.

"Oh, Elizabeth," he whispered, leaning his forehead against hers. "You have no idea how much I need you. Forgive me for being so rough; I know I should not…"

Barely able to speak, she put her hand to his cheek. "There is nothing to forgive, my love." In the darkness she could barely make out his face. "I assume you are less than happy that Colonel Fitzwilliam is staying here, but I will try to make sure my family does not embarrass itself too much before him; it should not be hard with both the Gardiners and Georgiana here."

Darcy gave a short laugh. "For once it makes no difference to me at all if your family behaves completely disgracefully."

She looked at him closely. "Then what is troubling you? And do not tell me it is nothing, since I will not believe you if you do."

"Elizabeth…" he paused, "sometimes there are things that are better not discussed."

"That may be true, but, as it happens, I seem to have a gift for jumping to the wrong conclusions when I am forced to guess at whatever it is that we are choosing not to discuss."

He was silent for a moment. "I cannot argue the point. If you wish, I will tell you, but please understand that I know that what I am about to say is completely without justification, and you have every right to be angry that I am even thinking it." He took a deep breath. "I… disliked seeing you laughing with my cousin; in fact I disliked it a great deal."

She stared at him, shocked. "Do you mean to suggest…?"

"I mean to suggest nothing except that I would happily toss him out on his ear to keep him away from you. As I said, I know full well that it is completely baseless, at least so far as you are concerned."

She considered this startling information for a few moments. "I am unsure what to say. There has never been anything between us in the past, and certainly there could not be now."

"Nothing on your part, perhaps—apart from having liked him better than you did me—but I cannot say the same for him," said Darcy darkly. "He was very taken with you at Rosings, and felt it necessary to tell me about it at length and repeatedly, an experience which I can assure you I did not enjoy. So when I see you happy in each other's company now… well, you can imagine, certainly." He might have added that, during the painful time after Rosings, one of his preferred methods of self-torture was to mull on the likelihood that Elizabeth would have happily accepted his cousin had *he* been the one to propose. The mere thought was enough to make him desperate to seek relief in Elizabeth's arms, and he embraced her fiercely, burying his face in her neck.

"I see," said Elizabeth, distracted by the exquisite sensations he was creating with his urgent caresses, but making a valiant attempt to continue the conversation. "Well, I cannot deny that there was a time I liked him better than you, but—" Her words were stopped as he captured her mouth, exploring it with a forceful and intoxicating thoroughness which threatened to deprive her of the possibility of rational speech. "…But as we both know, that was based on a misapprehension, and it is quite some time that I have loved you far more than I ever liked him." Having managed to say her piece, she finally allowed herself the guilty pleasure of surrendering once more to the passionate demands of his lips.

"He gave some thought to asking you to marry him, before deciding it was too imprudent financially," Darcy said, his hands beginning an insistent exploration of the curves of her body which threatened to overwhelm Elizabeth with fiery sensations.

"Well, under the circumstances, I am glad he did not; it would make things quite uncomfortable now, I would imagine," she said, struggling to stop her voice from shaking.

"Would you have refused him, then?" Darcy's voice was tense.

She hoped desperately that he was unable to tell just how thoroughly he had devastated her defenses with his passionate advances, and how much she wished he would not stop. "I truly cannot say what I would have done; I had only known him for three weeks, after all. I can only say that had I accepted him, I would have missed something far deeper."

He gripped her tightly. "Is that true? It is vain of me, I know, to want to be more important to you than any other man could have been."

"Have you never considered, my love, that I have always had a strong response to you? Even when I disliked you, I did so with a passion. Had I never met you, in all likelihood I could have found a man whom I could have learned to love, but I cannot believe it would have been with such depth, so... without reserve." She was amazed that she could speak so openly to him of her feelings, especially when her vulnerability to him was so great.

"Thank you," he responded, his voice muffled by her hair. "I know I should not need to hear such reassurance, but I do."

"Well, if you think I never have similar moments of anxiety about your regard, you are mistaken," she said softly.

He looked at her in astonishment. "You do? Why, in heaven's name, would you have the slightest doubt?"

She laughed and wound her arms around his neck. "Because I love you. Because I need you. Because I am all too human." She kissed him lingeringly, earning his full cooperation in the endeavor as he gathered her close, the touch of his lips becoming gentle and seductive.

"Because tomorrow cannot come soon enough," he added. He ran a finger across her lips, still somewhat swollen from his earlier ardor. "I have to warn you that no one seeing you tonight is going to be in doubt about what we have been doing out here." He trailed tantalizing kisses across her face.

"Do you think any of them will be surprised?"

"Well, if our guilt is to be obvious, I suppose that I might as well indulge myself a bit further," he replied, recapturing her lips. Giving in to an urge which had long tempted him, he ran his fingers deep into her hair, heedless of disrupting its careful styling. The intimacy of his touch caused her to arch herself against him, and he responded immediately by deepening the kiss, sending shivers of delight through her.

"You should send me away, my love, since I would happily stay here with you half the night," he said, demonstrating the truth of his words as he took his pleasure from her lips again.

She could not resist the opportunity, and said provocatively, "Well, you will need your rest for tomorrow."

He responded as she had known he would, pulling her to him hungrily and placing demanding kisses along her neck and shoulders until she was trembling with desire. "You need have no worries in that regard, madam," he responded. He tangled his fingers in her disheveled hair again, encouraging some silky locks to escape their close binding and fall along her flushed cheeks, and deeply enjoying seeing the results of his lovemaking in her appearance. With a mild possessive vindictiveness, he hoped that his cousin caught a good glimpse of her before she made herself presentable again.

She looked up at him with unconscious seductiveness, allowing her fingers to stray along the warm skin of his neck above his cravat. "I don't want you to go," she admitted softly.

He closed his eyes. He knew that she had no notion of

how near he was to taking advantage of her responsiveness and need, nor how powerfully his jealousy, justified or not, made him long to possess her. Carefully he removed her hands, and with a chaste kiss to each, joined them together and stepped away from her. In his most controlled voice, he said, "Elizabeth, no more provocation tonight, if you please."

She regarded him carefully. "I will bid you good night, then, Mr. Darcy."

"Good night, Miss Bennet." Recalling that it was the last time he would ever refer to her by that appellation, he smiled. "The next words I want to hear out of those lovely lips of yours are when you tell the parson 'I will' tomorrow morning." Unable to completely resist temptation, he kissed her once more with deep ardor, then took his leave.

Elizabeth sighed and wrapped her arms around herself as she watched him ride out of sight, then smiled and returned to the house.

⌘

"Mr. Darcy, you look particularly elegant this morning," said Jane over breakfast the following morning.

"Thank you, Mrs. Bingley. I hope your sister shares your opinion," he responded agreeably.

"Are you off to Longbourn this morning, then?"

Darcy busied himself with his food. "Yes, I expect to be there later, and then off to London this afternoon." Both Elizabeth and Bingley had been enjoying keeping Jane in the dark about the morning's events, and he would not be the one to spoil their amusement.

Jane looked concerned. "You are leaving today? Lizzy mentioned nothing of it—does she know?"

"Mmm, yes, she is well acquainted with my plans."

"We also have an engagement this morning, darling," said Bingley cheerfully, as if social calls on the day after one's wedding were nothing to be remarked on. "We will need to set out shortly after breakfast."

"Really? What is the occasion?"

"Ummm… it's a surprise," said Bingley, smiling broadly at Darcy.

"I take it that this is no surprise to you, Mr. Darcy."

Darcy stood. "Far be it from me to interfere between a new husband and wife, Mrs. Bingley. If you will excuse me," he said with a smile, taking his leave.

❦

Elizabeth was, as usual, the first of her family to come downstairs in the morning, and, after a brief turn about the grounds in lieu of her usual morning ramble, she sat down alone for a light breakfast. Within a few minutes she was joined by Georgiana and Kitty, followed soon thereafter by Colonel Fitzwilliam, who chose a seat next to her. She greeted him warmly, but found that she felt somewhat discomfited by his presence after Darcy's revelations of the previous night.

"I must admit that I was quite surprised to receive Darcy's letter that you and he were to be wed," he said in a measured manner. "I had guessed at Rosings that he admired you, but I must admit I had thought you less taken with him."

"That is, I take it, a tactful way of saying that it appeared that I disliked him heartily," Elizabeth said with a laugh.

"I certainly do not mean to imply that there was any… discord between you," he replied.

"Well, it is quite true; I did have an aversion to his company then, owing primarily to some misapprehensions about his behavior."

"I am glad you were able to resolve them, then. It is, indeed, a most prudent match for you."

Elizabeth looked sharply at him. Was he implying what she thought he was? Despite his neutral tone, she suspected a true concern on his part, as well as, perhaps, an element of the same feelings that had plagued Darcy about him. "Georgiana," she said with a cheerful smile, "Colonel Fitzwilliam is worried I am marrying your brother for his wealth, and that I have no true regard for him."

Georgiana and Kitty looked at each other and burst into peals of laughter. Colonel Fitzwilliam said hastily, "I certainly did not mean to imply anything of the sort, Miss Bennet; I am certain you would only marry for the best of reasons."

"Do not trouble yourself, sir; it is a perfectly reasonable conjecture on your part," she responded amiably. "It is, however, quite untrue."

Georgiana finally stopped laughing long enough to respond. "Oh, Richard, wait until you have a chance to see them together a bit more—they are so enamored of each other that the rest of us might as well be in China! I would venture they would not even notice if none of us came to the wedding!"

"They are *always* gazing into each other's eyes, or watching the other from across the room," Kitty added. "It can be quite embarrassing to see!"

"And then they go off by themselves again and again, and return looking so very calm and saintly, and no one is fooled at all, because they have been caught so often, but everyone knows that there is no winning an argument with either of them," said Georgiana.

Kitty giggled. "Do you remember what Father said yesterday? He looked at his watch and said, 'I wonder how long they will be this time!'"

"If I am ever caught in any misbehavior in the future, I will only have to remind Fitzwilliam of this time, and he will be unable to make any complaint!"

Elizabeth's cheeks were scarlet. "Georgiana, Kitty! Please excuse them, sir, they are very giddy today, I fear."

The girls looked at each other and laughed. "You asked what we thought," said Kitty.

"I shall certainly know better than to do so again!" cried Elizabeth.

Making little effort to hide a smile, Colonel Fitzwilliam

said, "Very well, I withdraw any objection; I am clearly not current with developments here."

Still mortally embarrassed, Elizabeth said, "I am sorry to have teased you, sir. My rather extreme change of heart is well known here, as is the very ill-kept secret that Mr. Darcy made me an offer of marriage while we were in Kent, and I refused him."

"So that is why he was in such a foul mood when we left! I have often wondered."

"Wasn't he awful?" agreed Georgiana.

"Monstrous," said the colonel. "Personally, I would rather spend my time with a maddened bear! Well, Miss Bennet, I am glad to know all is well between the two of you. I must admit I was finding it difficult to attribute mercenary motives to you given what I knew of you from Kent."

"I shall take that as a compliment," said Elizabeth. "Now, if you will excuse me, I am certain I can find something pressing to do somewhere where I will not be subject to more embarrassing stories!"

The sound of laughter followed her up the stairs.

Chapter 13

WHEN BINGLEY REJOINED DARCY an hour later at the church, he was still laughing over Jane's reaction to the news of the upcoming wedding. "She was all astonishment! Delighted, of course, but very confused, I must say. Just wait until I tell her about the honeymoon!"

"Married life clearly agrees with you, Bingley," Darcy responded to his boyish enthusiasm with a laugh.

"Oh, she is such an angel! I cannot begin to tell you," he said. "But what of you? Are you nervous? I could hardly hold myself together yesterday."

"Nervous?" Darcy raised an eyebrow. "Far from it! I feel relieved."

Bingley shook his head. "You *would* have to be different from every other bridegroom in history, wouldn't you?"

"Most bridegrooms have not suffered through the year that I have, then! I was nervous when I was fighting falling in love; I was unhappy pretending she did not matter to me after we left Hertfordshire. There were several good days, I admit, between when I first decided to propose to her and when she refused me, but then there were months of misery, then months of uncertainty. Then, since she accepted me, there has been the small matter of continual frustration—no, Bingley, I feel no anxiety today!"

"You *are* in a good mood!" said Bingley admiringly. "I believe that is more than I have ever heard from you on this subject."

"Yes, well, that is because it is over now," Darcy replied. "Or, more accurately, it will be if they ever decide to begin the service."

Bingley eyed him critically. "I do believe I detect just the slightest tinge of nervousness there, after all!"

Darcy fixed a hard stare on his friend. "I had been under the impression that your job today was to make things easier for me, but perhaps I was mistaken." Even in jest, however, he could not maintain a serious mien on this of all days, and broke into a smile.

"You'll do," said Bingley.

They heard a rustle from inside the nave, and the deacon gestured to them to enter and take their places. Darcy scanned the church, seeing the families assembled, and exchanged a warm smile with Georgiana, then was immediately distracted as he caught a glimpse of Elizabeth, lovelier than ever in a gown elegant in its simplicity, on her father's arm.

The service began, and as she came to stand at his left hand, he glanced at her to see a warm look in her beautiful eyes and a small playful smile hovering around her lips. He could not believe this moment for which he had hoped for so long was finally coming to pass.

The words of the service flowed past him almost unheeded as he found himself caught by thoughts of the indirect journey that had led them together to this moment. He was almost startled when he heard the parson say to him, "Wilt thou have this woman to thy wedded wife, to live together after God's ordinance in the holy estate of matrimony? Wilt thou love her, comfort her, honor, and keep her in sickness and in health; and, forsaking all other, keep thee only unto her, so long as ye both shall live?"

"I will," he said, his eyes speaking volumes more as he gazed at Elizabeth.

"Wilt thou have this man to thy wedded husband, to live together after God's ordinance in the holy estate of matrimony? Wilt thou obey him, and serve him, love, honor, and keep him in sickness and in health; and, forsaking all other, keep thee only unto him, so long as ye both shall live?"

Elizabeth's smile grew as she glanced at him, reminding him of his words the night before, as she said, "I will."

"Who giveth this woman to be married to this man?"

Mr. Bennet's eyes were suspiciously shiny as he kissed the cheek of his favorite daughter before giving her hand to the parson, who then placed it in Darcy's hand. He gave it a slight squeeze of reassurance, as his dark eyes captured her own. She felt that she could drown in that gaze, and sought to show him her own heart in the same manner as she listened to him repeat his vows. Then it was her turn, and she watched him take in a deep breath as she took him to be her wedded husband.

They might have been alone in the world as Darcy took his mother's wedding ring from the parson and slid it onto her finger. He could not immediately make himself say the words, so caught was he by the overwhelming sensation of fulfillment he felt as he held the ring there, and knew that at last she was his forever. His voice was low but firm as he said, each word charged with meaning, "With this ring I thee wed, with my body I thee worship, and with all my worldly goods I thee endow: in the Name of the Father, and of the Son, and of the Holy Ghost. Amen."

The parson had to cue them twice to kneel, which was little surprise to him as he had had ample opportunity over the previous two days to discover how very inattentive this particular couple could be. He recited the prayer over them, then joined their hands together again and pronounced, "Those whom God hath joined together let no man put asunder."

The words echoed in Darcy's mind as his hand tightened on hers. His lovely Elizabeth! How long he had waited for this, and through what trials—but it was all worth it now. The joy that filled his heart was all-consuming. He could think of nothing but the warm look in her eyes, the smile on her lips, and the many years he would have to enjoy them.

⁂

The wedding breakfast was a pleasant but brief affair, since the newlyweds wished to depart early enough to reach London while there was still daylight remaining. The time went very quickly, and almost before she realized it, Elizabeth was standing outside Longbourn bidding her family farewell before setting off in the handsome coach-and-four at the gate. The farewells were not protracted, as the Darcys planned to stop by Longbourn briefly en route to Pemberley the following week to collect Georgiana.

Elizabeth looked up with slight shock at the coach, which was certainly the most elegant conveyance she had ever ridden in, as Darcy handed her in. She settled herself gingerly on the well-padded seat as Darcy entered and sat opposite her, as propriety dictated. With a glance at her, he signaled the driver to depart.

They had not gone far beyond Longbourn when Darcy, smiling, said, "Well, Mrs. Darcy?"

Elizabeth raised an eyebrow. "Well, Mr. Darcy?"

"Would it be indelicate to inquire as to the cause of that amused smile upon your face?"

"In fact, I was contemplating what a disappointment I would be to Miss Bingley. When I saw this lovely coach, I realized that I have been failing throughout our courtship to pay any heed to the question of your wealth. And since I have been thinking only of being with you, I have managed to utterly ignore the fact that I have no idea where we are going, since I have never so much as asked which part of London your house is in, nor what it is like. I believe that Miss Bingley would find my priorities quite unacceptable."

Darcy smiled. "*Our* house," he corrected.

"*That* will take some getting used to," said Elizabeth. "You will have to forgive me if I cannot take it in all at once."

"Surely you cannot have forgotten already—'with all my worldly goods I thee endow?'" he teased. "Come now, you can manage it. Just try saying it—our house, our coach, our finances."

"Our quarrels, our embarrassing relations," Elizabeth shot back cheerfully.

"Don't tell me you have already forgotten the part where you promised to obey me," he said with mock seriousness.

"Completely and totally forgotten," she agreed. "However, I have an excellent memory for the 'love and cherish' part."

"In that case, perhaps you would not be overly shocked if I asked to sit next to you instead of all the way over here?"

"I must admit, I do not shock as easily as I did a few months ago. I fear you have had a pernicious influence on me."

Darcy laughed as he carefully shifted himself across the coach. He put his arm around Elizabeth, who promptly nestled in close to him. "Mmm. I think I am going to like being married to you," he said.

"Well, if not, you have picked an unfortunate time to realize it, sir!"

He kissed her hair. "I am completely satisfied, my love."

"I am relieved to hear it," she said. Reaching down, she drew out a small package. "I have something for you," she added, a bit shyly, as she handed it to him.

"For me?" he inquired, surprised.

"Yes, it is a… umm, replacement. When I left Lambton that day, I took something of yours with me that I never returned."

"Besides my heart?" He smiled warmly at her.

"That I cannot replace, nor would I have any wish to do so! This is something much simpler."

Opening the package, he discovered that it held a hand-kerchief, embroidered with his initials within a small circle of flowers. Elizabeth reached over and touched the flowers. "They are forget-me-nots and sweet williams," she explained. "Do you remember that day we walked in the garden and spoke of flowers for each other?"

"Vividly." He took her hand in his. "Thank you, my dearest. I shall treasure it, not least as a sign that you thought of me while we were apart. But you also left something behind in Lambton."

"Besides *my* heart?"

He could not resist kissing her lingeringly. "Besides that." From his pocket he produced a neatly folded handkerchief that she recognized as her own. "It has been my constant companion, and no, you may not have it back. I have grown quite fond of it."

"Then it is yours, my love. You may have noticed that I chose to replace, and not return, yours. I think I shall put that under the category of those worldly goods with which you endowed me earlier."

Darcy raised an eyebrow at her. "You are willing to accept the handkerchief, but not the house, the coach, or the finances?" he teased. "Will you always be this easy to please?"

"Quite likely, since the only thing I truly want is you, and have no need for your worldly goods. Although I might make an exception for the grounds at Pemberley, as I am looking forward to many long walks through them."

"The handkerchief and the grounds at Pemberley? That seems a reasonable enough request. They are yours, along with my heart, *and* all my other worldly goods," he said playfully. "So, would you like to hear about *our* London house or not?"

"I suppose I must, mustn't I?"

"Let me see… it is about a block from the docks, a dark, drafty place. The roof leaks, and—" His teasing was interrupted in a most pleasant way.

"There is only one crucial thing I need to know about this terrible place," said Elizabeth as she drew back. "How will the housekeeper respond to my presence?"

"Mrs. Adams? She will take one look at you and decide where you will fit in her extremely organized household, and I strongly suggest gracious submission on your part. Mrs. Reynolds at Pemberley at least allows the illusion that

I am—or we are—in charge, but there is no question as to who runs the household in London."

"I find it hard to picture *you* submitting graciously, Fitzwilliam!"

Hard to picture! What did she think he had been doing since he met her? Well, perhaps some of it involved submitting less than graciously. There were so many possible responses to her comment, nearly all of them provocative, and he knew full well where that would lead. Desire rose in him, and he briefly regretted sitting so close to her, but managed to stay still by sheer willpower. He had strict plans for his behavior on this particular day, and, in deference to his desire to retain some degree of sanity when they reached London, those plans did not include permitting any passionate interludes while they were alone in a coach for two hours. Finally he forced himself to say, "I know better than to argue with Mrs. Adams!"

She tilted her head to look up at him with a bewitching smile. "I shall look forward to seeing that."

The temptation to kiss her was nearly overpowering. Sighing, he settled himself back for what was clearly going to seem like a very long journey.

Darcy's townhouse did not disappoint; it demonstrated the same elegance and good taste which had characterized Pemberley. Elizabeth could still not quite credit that she would be living in such lovely homes, and felt disconcerted as she was greeted by each servant in turn—and there were so many of them!—as Mrs. Darcy. The alarming Mrs. Adams turned out to be a plump, motherly woman who greeted Darcy with obvious affection and welcomed Elizabeth warmly.

After a brief period of refreshment, Darcy took Elizabeth on a tour of the house to which she attended with great interest, though she was continually more distracted by thoughts of the night that lay ahead. She was not surprised to find an extensive and clearly well-used library; she could picture Darcy spending hours there. She paused in the dining room, where a portrait of a lovely woman bearing a distinct resemblance to Georgiana graced the wall over the mantle. She looked over her shoulder at Darcy. "Is that your mother?" she asked.

He came up behind her and slid his arms around her waist. "Yes, that was painted shortly after she married my father. She would have liked you."

"I wish I could have met her," she said, leaning back against him. She relaxed in his arms, but Darcy's response was far from relaxation—he had been suffering in silence quite long enough. He bent his head and began to press gentle, slow kisses on her exposed neck. She gasped, involuntarily arching her neck to allow him better access. She whispered his name with longing as he moved onward to explore the hollows of her shoulder. She felt a deep desire rise in her as he allowed his hands to caress her, and struggled to reach his lips with hers in an effort to gain some relief.

Their mouths met with a deep hunger, and Darcy pulled away sooner than she would have wished. She looked up into his eyes, dark with passion, as he released her and whispered, "Soon, my love, soon."

Elizabeth blushed a fiery red at his acknowledgement of the night to come, unaware that he was thinking if he touched her for one minute longer, he would lose all his good intentions and carry her upstairs immediately.

God, but he loved making her want him! And he had plans to do a great deal more of it. Later.

Mrs. Adams materialized in the doorway, making Elizabeth wonder in embarrassment how long she might have been waiting for a decent moment to walk in. "Mrs. Darcy, I was wondering if you would like me to show you to your rooms so that you can refresh yourself before supper?"

Elizabeth consented, but was aware of a pair of dark eyes that followed her intently as she left.

❧

Supper was a somewhat forced affair, with both Darcy and Elizabeth trying to keep a light conversation going while their minds were quite occupied elsewhere. Sudden pauses would occur, accompanied by a coloring of her cheeks, but for the most part they successfully talked of their plans for London and Pemberley with great perseverance. Afterward Darcy requested the pleasure of a song at the pianoforte, in which Elizabeth was happy to oblige him, not least because it provided an opportunity for distraction from her thoughts of what lay ahead. Shortly thereafter, she came to the conclusion that this period of waiting was only making her more nervous, and announced her intent to retire for the night.

She met her new maid, who assisted her in her preparations quietly and unobtrusively. *Another thing to get used to, my own maid,* she thought philosophically as she dressed herself in her silk nightgown and matching dressing gown, a gift from her aunt Gardiner for the occasion. As she brushed out her hair, she pondered Mrs. Gardiner's other gift, a gentle but frank discussion of what this night would involve. It was rather difficult to picture, she decided, then recalled her aunt's words—*It may seem quite confusing, but remember, my dear, to trust your husband; he loves you and will be gentle.* She was glad now she and Darcy had taken some liberties ahead of this day, so at least it would not all be foreign. Some of his kisses had led to startling enough effects on their own.

In the next room, Darcy was similarly preoccupied as he carefully reviewed in his mind his plans for the night. He had given the question of how to approach Elizabeth a great deal of thought—after all, it had been one of his favorite subjects for consideration for some time—and had concluded that his greatest challenge was to be patient and gentle when his every instinct was craving immediate satisfaction. He had been present over the years at enough late-night conversations at his club—not to mention a few carefully placed words of advice from Mr. Gardiner—to be aware that for a protected, gently bred young woman the wedding night offered potential for an unpleasant experience, and he was determined that his passionate and responsive Elizabeth should have no reason after this night to be any less passionate or responsive.

Taking his planning down to great detail, he had decided that it might be a little too disconcerting for Elizabeth to see him this first time in his nightshirt and robes. He had determined that he would approach her in his shirt and breeches, which might be less shocking.

Unfortunately, there was only so far that planning could take him, and then he had to face the uncertain realities of the situation. *This is it, man,* he told himself, *this is what you have been waiting for these many months*. Taking a deep breath, he walked over to the adjoining door to her room and knocked lightly.

Hearing her soft voice bidding him enter, he opened the door to see her sitting at her vanity brushing out her hair. The sight of her in her nightclothes, her dark hair loose around her shoulders as he had so often imagined, nearly made him dizzy with desire at the thought of being alone with her and uninterrupted. He leaned a hand against the doorframe for support as he drank in the picture for a moment, then walked over to stand behind her chair, resting his hands lightly on her shoulders.

They regarded one another in the mirror for a moment, then Elizabeth smiled and placed her hand affectionately over one of his, and was rewarded by the warm look in his eyes. He looked devastatingly attractive unencumbered by waistcoat, tailcoat, and cravat, his shirt open slightly at the neck, and she found that her mouth was becoming dry.

He ran his fingers gently through her hair as he had so long desired to do. "You look very beautiful tonight, my love," he said softly. He gathered her hair in his hand, and, moving it to one side, leaned over and gently kissed the nape of her neck.

It was unfair that his every touch had such power to stir her, she thought as he moved his lips along her exposed neck. Sensation built up in Elizabeth as he enjoyed the taste of her delicate skin. His mind tried to leap ahead to all the other ways he planned to enjoy her, but he firmly reined himself in, the only visible sign of his struggle being a slight tightening of his hands on her shoulder. With deliberation, he gently moved aside her robe to expose part of her shoulder in a symbolic disrobement, attending carefully to see how she responded. She remained still, but in the mirror he could see that her lips were parted, and he could feel the shallowness of her breathing. Pleased, he allowed his lips to explore the area his fingers had discovered.

Elizabeth, meanwhile, was astonished by the sensations he was creating. She had thought herself already aware of how powerfully his touch could move her, but as he had slipped his fingers under the edge of her nightgown, the depth of her awareness of his touch had threatened to overwhelm her. She gripped the arms of her chair, and Darcy, sensing her response, allowed his lips to linger in the hollows of her shoulder.

She shivered, and he raised his head to look at her in concern, hoping she was feeling no fear. His eyes silently asked her for permission to continue, and in response, unable to tolerate being only the passive recipient of his touch any longer, she turned her head and drew his mouth down to hers with a hunger that could not be denied. He tasted the delight of her lips, and incapable of being as patient for her touch as he wished, drew her to her feet and into his arms. She felt a shock at her awareness of his body against hers, augmented by the absence of his coat; now she could feel the shape and strength of his broad shoulders, and it aroused her profoundly and made her long for more.

"Elizabeth, my Elizabeth," he murmured as he once again took possession of her mouth. As if able to hear her desires, his hands slid down to the belt of her dressing gown and untied it with fingers that felt suddenly clumsy. Unable to deny himself, he slipped his hands between her robe and her nightgown and caressed her back, delighting in the feel of the nooks and crannies that the fine fabric did not disguise.

With a moan of pleasure, she arched herself against him. He continued to stroke his hands along her body, exploring curves he had only dreamed of. There was no more room for fear; she felt driven by pure sensation. She whispered his name in a plea for she knew not what, and, sensing her surrender to her own desires, his own self-control slipped even further. He stepped back just far enough to lift the robe off her shoulders and let it slide to the ground, allowing him to admire her form, little disguised by her nightgown.

The scrutiny of his eyes was not enough to meet Elizabeth's longing. Feeling momentarily bereft of his touch, her instincts led her to run her hands down his chest, arousing him powerfully, until, no longer able to resist his own need to feel her touch, he covered her hands with his own and slid them under his shirt. Hearing her gasp, the thought penetrated his passion-hazed mind that perhaps he had pushed her too quickly, but as her hands began their own delightful exploration, it became clear the only shock was one of intense pleasure. Elizabeth, stunned by the intimate sensation of his warm skin under her fingers, let her hands explore his back as she pressed herself against him, her body craving the pleasure only he could give her.

The sweet torture of her touch aroused him even beyond what he had expected. His need for her grew as he felt her soft body against him, and, knowing he could wait no longer, he gave in to temptation and finally let his hands move upward and untied the drawstring of the last remaining impediment to his beloved Elizabeth.

❧

Darcy awoke the next morning to a pleasant feeling of warmth. His heart stilled as he saw Elizabeth's sleeping face next to his, a small smile of contentment curving her lips, and her dark hair spread across the pillow and drifting onto his chest. *It is not often one has the opportunity to see one's dreams turn into reality*, he thought dreamily. With his eyes he traced the lines of her beloved face, and thought how privileged he was to be able to wake up with such a bewitching woman beside him.

Falling asleep with her in his arms had been quite extraordinary as well, he thought. His mind drifted to the events of the previous night, and he smiled to think of the delight they had found together, the intense pleasure he had taken in helping her to discover the surprises her body had in store for her. Her responsiveness had been everything he hoped for and more, and it was with the greatest of satisfaction that he recalled their explorations and how they led to the moment when her desire and pleasure had equaled his own. The look of wonder on her face after he had satisfied her was one he would never forget.

Even more powerful was the knowledge that they now truly belonged to one another. After all the misunderstandings, the pain, and the separations, Elizabeth was finally his, and there could be no going back. No more fears she would somehow disappear if he said or did the wrong thing—now, if they had a conflict, they would have to work it out together, for better or for worse. Having Elizabeth to share his life was the greatest gift he could imagine.

Her eyes fluttered open as he watched. She colored as she realized where she was, and how comfortable she felt with her limbs entangled with his. It was a moment before she felt ready to meet his eyes, but when she did, she found them full of warmth and affection.

"Good morning, Mrs. Darcy," he said softly, the appellation a reminder that he could expect this pleasure for the rest of his life.

"Good morning to you, Mr. Darcy," she responded with a sleepy smile.

"Indeed it is a very good morning," he agreed, giving her a light kiss.

She nestled closer to him, astonished anew by the exquisite sensation of his skin against hers. What a night of discovery it had been for her, as Darcy had tantalizingly led her each step of the way to places she had never dreamed of. To think that she had believed that she had already experienced the deepest extent of desire! Nothing had prepared her for what he had unleashed in her, or for the pleasure and satisfaction that followed. Her eyes grew dark with the remembrance of it.

His awareness of Elizabeth's body against his was rousing similar feelings in Darcy. His hand, seemingly of its own accord, began to slide along her curves. Their eyes met, sharing messages between them, until their mouths joined with a deep passion. He experienced not so much a gradual building as a sudden onslaught of desire, as if the satisfactions of the night before had never existed, and he could tell from her response that she was feeling a similar intensity. His need communicated itself to her as he pulled her to him and captured her mouth with a burning urgency that matched her own, and Elizabeth saw there were yet more new experiences in store for her.

IT WAS SNOWING VERY lightly when they left Pemberley for Lambton. After several days of poor weather kept them restricted indoors, Elizabeth was longing for a chance to set foot in the outside world. Mrs. Gardiner had expressed an interest in visiting one of her Lambton friends, and Elizabeth was interested in finding some new millinery, so an outing was decided upon. Darcy decided at the last moment to join them, though how much was due to a desire for the company of his wife, and how much represented an excess of exposure to the post-Christmas exuberance of the Gardiner children could not be said.

The Darcys had visited Lambton on several occasions since their return to Pemberley. Although the Darcy family never before favored Lambton with their custom, Elizabeth had early established a preference for the small market town owing to her previous familiarity with it. Her inclination was reinforced by the friendly behavior of the inhabitants, who took personal pride in the new Mrs. Darcy as the niece of a former Lambton resident, and, should anyone in the town have forgotten that she had met with Mr. Darcy on more than one occasion in their village, any number of people would have reminded them of the fact immediately. The value of a mistress of Pemberley who brought her family to their village could not be underestimated, either.

Certain of the village residents had therefore seen it as their business to find out more about the goings-on in the Darcy family, and, in cultivating their acquaintance with members of the staff at Pemberley, had been able to report back that Mr. Darcy was considered to be exceedingly enamored of his lively new wife, and much more cheerful and less proud than was his former wont. This intelligence being spread rapidly throughout the town, Mr. Darcy was bemused to discover that he was being greeted with smiles of amused indulgence from the villagers whenever he accompanied his wife to Lambton. Though he professed bafflement with the change, Elizabeth suspected that he surreptitiously enjoyed being the recipient of this kind of attention, so unlike any he had received in the past.

When Elizabeth finished her business in the town, she found it still wanted an hour until the time Mrs. Gardiner was to rejoin them. Rather than hurry her aunt's visit, Darcy suggested they might stop at the Lambton Inn for something warm to drink. This being agreeable to her, they proceeded to the inn where the proprietor, feeling the Darcys might prefer more privacy than the main room offered, showed them to the private sitting room Elizabeth remembered well from her last visit.

Elizabeth looked around at the familiar paneled walls and heavy furniture. Turning to her husband with a smile, she asked, "Do you remember the last time we were here together?"

"Vividly. I lived on the memory of those moments for weeks."

"And now, not half a year later, here we are again."

"But in a condition much different from where we left off, and far preferable, I must say."

It was indeed far preferable, Elizabeth thought, reflecting on how content she had been since their marriage. Pemberley, while still new to her, was beginning to feel like her home; Georgiana was becoming a true sister, and the staff at Pemberley had welcomed her. If Mrs. Reynolds possessed any qualms about the young woman her master had brought home, she overcame them when she saw the joy she brought him, and the liveliness, absent from Pemberley these many years since old Mr. Darcy passed away, that she added to the household. She remarked to Elizabeth on one occasion how much more like his old self as a boy Mr. Darcy seemed. Elizabeth was also quite certain the housekeeper was pleased by the Gardiners' Christmas visit, since it meant the halls of Pemberley were ringing with children's laughter and Christmas spirit again.

"And with far better understanding of one another, I should hope," she added.

"I believe you could safely say that," he agreed.

"As I recall, you had some difficulty believing I was serious in my regard for you," she teased.

"That was only because I was so afraid of losing you again," Darcy said, thinking back to the anxieties of their courtship.

"I am not so easy to be rid of," she said. "Besides, I could never leave you to the mercy of the fashionable ladies of the *ton*!" This had become a regular source of teasing between the two since Elizabeth had finally come to understand why, with all the finest society ladies to choose from, he had fallen in love with a mere country gentleman's daughter. She now questioned why anyone had ever thought that he might wed a society lady, since it had become obvious that a country girl was what he would have wanted all along, had he given the matter any thought. A wife who longed for the social delights of London would have made him miserable; in fact, when they decided to forgo completely the pleasures of the Season in London this year, and to spend the winter at Pemberley instead, Darcy had shown nothing but relief, and had even been heard on occasion to regret that they could not do the same next year, since their presence would be required for Georgiana's first Season.

"There are certain things that are quite unchanged, though," Darcy said meaningfully.

"And what, pray tell, do you have in mind, sir?" asked Elizabeth impertinently, knowing full well where his thoughts were headed.

With a teasing smile, he drew her onto his lap. "I still spend a great deal of time thinking about how much I want to kiss you," he said softly in her ear, and proceeded to do just that.

Elizabeth wound her arms around his neck and, having learned a good deal in the last two months about how to gain her husband's attention, ran her finger lightly under the very edge of his cravat and began skillfully torturing him with light kisses along his face. "Elizabeth," he moaned, retaliating by trailing kisses along her neck before recapturing her mouth with a series of passionate kisses that left her breathless. "Must you do this to me when we are five miles from home?"

"You started it," she pointed out wickedly, redoubling her efforts. "Shall I stop, then?"

"You know the answer to that," he growled, and stemmed her laughter by the most efficient means available to him.

It was then that Nan, the serving girl, appeared in the doorway carrying a tray with their coffees, only to find the Master and Mistress of Pemberley locked in a passionate embrace. Apparently the Pemberley staff had not been exaggerating after all about how often they discovered the Darcys in a compromising position! She retreated on tiptoe, closing the door quietly behind her. With a broad smile, she headed toward the kitchen where she knew she would have an eager audience for her tidings.

Acknowledgments

This book would never have been completed without the help and support of many people. My thanks to the readers who read it as a work in progress and offered helpful comments. The staff and participants at The Republic of Pemberley website provided the first home for this story and the original idea for the Pemberley Variations. Ellen Pickels provided keen editing eyes and invaluable technical support.

I must also thank my extraordinary editor, Deb Werksman, for her belief in my work, as well as my agent, Lauren Abramo, for her patience and support. Danielle Jackson of Sourcebooks walked me through the publicity minefields.

Last, but never least, I want to thank my beloved husband, David, for understanding and tolerating my anxiety while writing my first novel; my children, Rebecca and Brian, for not saying their mom was crazy (okay, well, they didn't say it *much*); and all the wayward children who have made our home your own—you know who you are—for making sure my life is never dull. I love you all.

About the Author

Abigail Reynolds is a lifelong Jane Austen enthusiast and a physician. In addition to writing, she has a part-time private practice and enjoys spending time with her family. Originally from upstate New York, she studied Russian, theater, and marine biology before deciding to attend medical school. She began writing *Pride and Prejudice* Variations in 2001 to spend more time with her favorite Jane Austen characters. Encouragement from fellow Austen fans persuaded her to continue asking "What if...?", which led to four other *Pride and Prejudice* Variations and her contemporary novel, *The Man Who Loved Pride and Prejudice*. She is currently at work on a sequel to *Mr. Darcy's Obsession*, as well as the companion novels to *The Man Who Loved Pride and Prejudice*. She lives in Wisconsin with her husband, two teenage children, and a menagerie of pets.

Mr. Fitzwilliam Darcy:
THE LAST MAN IN THE WORLD
A *Pride and Prejudice* Variation
ABIGAIL REYNOLDS

What if Elizabeth had accepted Mr. Darcy the first time he asked?

In Jane Austen's *Pride and Prejudice*, Elizabeth Bennet tells the proud Mr. Fitzwilliam Darcy that she wouldn't marry him if he were the last man in the world. But what if circumstances conspired to make her accept Darcy the first time he proposes? In this installment of Abigail Reynolds' acclaimed *Pride and Prejudice* Variations, Elizabeth agrees to marry Darcy against her better judgment, setting off a chain of events that nearly brings disaster to them both. Ultimately, Darcy and Elizabeth will have to work together on their tumultuous and passionate journey to make a success of their ill-timed marriage.

What readers are saying:

"A highly original story, immensely satisfying."

"Anyone who loves the story of Darcy and Elizabeth will love this variation."

"I was hooked from page one."

"A refreshing new look at what might have happened if..."

"Another good book to curl up with... I never wanted to put it down..."

978-1-4022-2947-3
$14.99 US/$18.99 CAN/£7.99 UK

Loving Mr. Darcy: Journeys Beyond Pemberley
SHARON LATHAN

"A romance that transcends time." —*The Romance Studio*

Darcy and Elizabeth embark on the journey of a lifetime

Six months into his marriage to Elizabeth Bennet, Darcy is still head over heels in love, and each day offers more opportunities to surprise and delight his beloved bride. Elizabeth has adapted to being the Mistress of Pemberley, charming everyone she meets and handling her duties with grace and poise. Just when it seems life can't get any better, Elizabeth gets the most wonderful news. The lovers leave the serenity of Pemberley, traveling through the sumptuous landscape of Regency England, experiencing the lavish sights, sounds, and tastes around them. With each day come new discoveries as they become further entwined, body and soul.

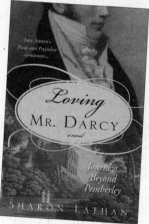

What readers are saying:

"Darcy's passion for love and life with Lizzy is brought to the forefront and captured beautifully."

"Sharon Lathan is a wonderful writer... I believe that Jane Austen herself would love this story as much as I did."

"The historical backdrop of the book is unbelievable—I actually felt like I could see all the places where the Darcys traveled."

"Truly captures the heart of Darcy & Elizabeth! Very well written and totally hot!"

978-1-4022-1741-8 • $14.99 US/ $18.99 CAN/ £7.99 UK

My Dearest Mr. Darcy

SHARON LATHAN

Darcy is more deeply in love with his wife than ever

As the golden summer draws to a close and the Darcys look ahead to the end of their first year of marriage, Mr. Darcy could never have imagined his love could grow even deeper with the passage of time. Elizabeth is unpredictable and lively, pulling Darcy out of his stern and serious demeanor with her teasing and temptation.

But surprising events force the Darcys to weather absence and illness, and to discover whether they can find a way to build a bond of everlasting love and desire…

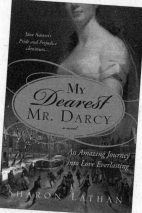

978-1-4022-1742-5
$14.99 US/$18.99 CAN/£7.99 UK

To Conquer
Mr. Darcy

By ABIGAIL REYNOLDS

What if? Instead of disappearing from Elizabeth Bennet's life after she refused his offer of marriage, Mr. Darcy had stayed and tried to change her mind?

What if? Lizzy, as she gets to know Darcy, finds him undeniably attractive and her impulses win out over her sense of propriety?

What if? Madly in love and mutually on fire, their passion anticipates their wedding?

In *To Conquer Mr. Darcy*, instead of avoiding Elizabeth after his ill-fated marriage proposal, Mr. Darcy follows her back to Hertfordshire, planning to prove to her he is a changed man and worthy of her love. And little by little, Elizabeth begins to find the man she despised becoming irresistible…

978-1-4022-3730-0 • $6.99 U.S./$8.99 CAN/£3.99 UK

Wickham's Diary

Amanda Grange

Jane Austen's quintessential bad boy has his say…

Enter the clandestine world of the cold-hearted Wickham…

…in the pages of his private diary. Always aware of the inferiority of his social status compared to his friend Fitzwilliam Darcy, Wickham chases wealth and women in an attempt to attain the power he lusts for. But as Wickham gambles and cavorts his way through his funds, Darcy still comes out on top.

But now Wickham has found his chance to seduce the young Georgiana Darcy, which will finally secure the fortune—and the revenge—he's always dreamed of…

Praise for Amanda Grange:

"Amanda Grange has taken on the challenge of reworking a much loved romance and succeeds brilliantly." —*Historical Novels Review*

"Amanda Grange is a writer who tells an engaging, thoroughly enjoyable story!" —*Romance Reader at Heart*

Available April 2011
978-1-4022-5186-3
$12.99 US

In the Arms of Mr. Darcy
SHARON LATHAN

If only everyone could be as happy as they are…

Darcy and Elizabeth are as much in love as ever—even more so as their relationship matures. Their passion inspires everyone around them, and as winter turns to spring, romance blossoms around them.

Confirmed bachelor Richard Fitzwilliam sets his sights on a seemingly unattainable, beautiful widow; Georgiana Darcy learns to flirt outrageously; the very flighty Kitty Bennet develops her first crush, and Caroline Bingley meets her match.

But the path of true love never does run smooth, and Elizabeth and Darcy are kept busy navigating their friends and loved ones through the inevitable separations, misunderstandings, misgivings, and lovers' quarrels to reach their own happily ever afters…

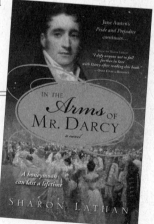

"If you love *Pride and Prejudice* sequels then this series should be on the top of your list!"
—*Royal Reviews*

"Sharon really knows how to make Regency come alive." —*Love Romance Passion*

978-1-4022-3699-0
$14.99 US/$17.99 CAN/£9.99 UK

The Other Mr. Darcy

Pride and Prejudice CONTINUES...

Monica Fairview

"A lovely story... a joy to read."
—*Bookishly Attentive*

Unpredictable courtships appear to run in the Darcy family...

When Caroline Bingley collapses to the floor and sobs at Mr. Darcy's wedding, imagine her humiliation when she discovers that a stranger has witnessed her emotional display. Miss Bingley, understandably, resents this gentleman very much, even if he is Mr. Darcy's American cousin. Mr. Robert Darcy is as charming as Mr. Fitzwilliam Darcy is proud, and he is stunned to find a beautiful young woman weeping broken-heartedly at his cousin's wedding. Such depth of love, he thinks, is rare and precious. For him, it's love at first sight...

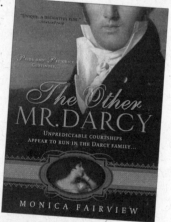

978-1-4022-2513-0
$14.99 US/$18.99 CAN/£7.99 UK

"An intriguing concept...
a delightful ride in the park."
—*Austenprose*